The Opium Eater and Other Stories

The Opium Eater
and
Other Stories

by
Iqbal Ahmad

Cormorant Books

Published with the assistance of the Canada Council, the Ontario Arts Council, and Secretary of State for Multiculturalism.

The author wishes to acknowledge previous publications of "The Opium Eater" in *The Atlantic Monthly,* "Time to Go" in *The Canadian Forum,* "The Kumbh Fair" in *The Fiddlehead,* "Grandma" in *The Literary Review* (New Jersey), "The Clown" in *The South Asian Review,* "The Custard-Apple Hunt" in *The Illustrated Weekly of India,* and "Ahmad Din Goes Hunting" in *Descant.*

Cover from a detail from *Casa Matta,* an oil on canvas (1984) by Martin Honisch, courtesy of the artist, from the collection of Amelia Ayre.

Published by Cormorant Books, RR 1, Dunvegan, Ontario, Canada K0C 1J0

Printed and bound in Canada.

Canadian Cataloguing in Publication Data

Ahmad, Iqbal, 1921-

The opium eater and other stories

ISBN 0-920953-74-3

I. Title.

PS8551.H64064 1992   C813' .54   C92-090084-4
PR9199.3.A45064 1992

For Farhat

CONTENTS

1

Sanki died suddenly. The news did not surprise me; he was so dangerously thin that I knew anything could carry him off. Besides, lately he had picked up the habit of eating opium. In the long winter evenings he scarcely ever left his room—a dingy hole where he lived by himself in hostile seclusion. Once or twice I invaded his privacy and found him dozing in a corner under the influence of the drug.

He had never liked people, and for company's sake he kept a parrot. His companion shared his habit. Perched on a rod, half asleep, it would nod violently from time to time. The miserable bird got so used to the opium that it would set up a terrible squawking if its pellet were not forthcoming at the appointed hour. The drug had a curious effect on it. First, it lost the glossiness of its plumage; then it grew scruffy and bald in patches and ultimately shed all its feathers. It looked obscene in its nakedness. But it was a good companion—at least Sanki thought so; and in its sober moments, it could recite a few couplets of Hafiz.

Sanki used to tell me that there were worlds beyond the clouds, even beyond the stars, and he would give glowing descriptions of them. After he had had the black pellet, he would feel his consciousness gradually dissolve into the mist, into the universal twilight. He felt he was the dark, vapoury blood of the world. Visions rose before him, visions of rolling countries of twilight, warm and cloud-big men and women and the mute, slow, ecstatic mingling of their bodies. To me, it would seem that the scientists were wrong when they spoke of the utter coldness and darkness of outer space; and the warm eloquence of the opium eater would incline me toward poetry. The winding procession of stars seemed like village girls coming from a well; star-cities rose far, far out in the depth of space.

'My friend,' I would say, 'you are a poet. Why don't you write about these things? Show us the soul taking a holiday, riding away on the tail of a comet, bathing in the canals of Mars, sleeping in the caves of the moon.'

'Oh! Are there caves and canals up there?'

'Yes, so the scientists say.'

'I shall see the next time,' he would say. 'I can always verify these things, you know; it's my domain.'

I met him the first time five years ago at a cricket match. Tall and lean, he stood at the wicket for half an hour without swinging once, and our patience ran out. His long, lank hair fell in a fringe over his eyes. He did not bother to brush the fringe aside, even when he was batting; he preferred to peep through the black threads. His white shirt was held together in the front with black shoelaces.

Later, at the lunch table, an unceasing stream of delightful chatter flowed from his lips, and we gathered in a ring around him. He consumed half a dozen cups of tea, smoked like a chimney, and left the eatables untouched. On a request, he recited an elegy of his own composition in Persian. I marvelled at his command of the language. The couplets flowed smoothly, but the imagery was bizarre and fantastic in the extreme, and there was a deliberate touch of the grotesque. It was as if a sculptor, having made a beautiful statue, slashed off the nose for a finishing touch. Afterward, he dashed off in a great hurry, the fringe of his hair jiggling up and down on his forehead.

When I saw him again, I found him sitting at a betel-seller's shop near his drab hotel. There was an Urdu translation of *Hamlet* under his arm. He showed me the book, which bore many betel-juice marks on it. 'Natrajan, the university lecturer, gave it to me,' he said. 'He has been to England and often speaks to me of those people and their ways. I read it and found it first-rate poetry. But a suspicion has crept into my mind.' Sanki paused for dramatic effect. 'I think this Shakespeare was not English.'

'What!' I exclaimed.

'Yes, he was not English. I can't imagine how poetry can be written in a country where people love beer and have no sun. I am told that even those poets whose identities cannot be questioned had to go to Italy to write their poetry. But about this impostor, this Shakespeare, I am pretty certain.'

'Well, if he wasn't English, what was he?'

'Persian, a Persian gypsy in disguise to avoid the law, and the English had sense enough not to expose him.'

I was astonished. 'How can you say that?'

'Look at the quality of the poetry. It's the highest,

it's Persian. You can always tell by the taste. You know, the art of poetry is very close to the art of brewing, and the Persians are masters of both. Hafiz was the best of brewers. You have heard of the wine of Shiraz? Persian poetry was distilled from wine. From the translations of English poetry I have seen, I always judged it was distilled from beer. But this Shakespeare, he tastes of the grape; yes, the grape.'

Sanki continued moodily: 'You know, my soul dances like a dervish when I read Hafiz. I wish you could see its joyful dance—like the sunbeam of a child's smile. Well, this Shakespeare too moves my soul to dance. There is no doubt of it, he was a Persian. And look at the name. It's a corruption of Sheikh Peero, a common name among the gypsies of Iran even to this day. Don't you agree?'

'I seem to,' I said. And for a moment I really did.

'The English are a remarkable people,' Sanki continued reflectively. 'Look at them, nothing but a hoax! Look at the language. I am told fragments of various languages were put together and confidently called English. Look at the people. Exiles and invaders every one. But when the crowd got sizable, they were called English. Nothing but raw material, that's all, imported from every corner of the earth. English language, English people, English goods, English wealth—tell me, are they really English? Not one. They have made a legend more powerful than the dreams of Firdausi. And by the way, Natrajan agrees with me that in England there is nothing English but the weather.'

I heard him with a strange kind of admiration and joy, and I said, 'My friend, you speak like a scholar.'

Sanki shuddered. 'For heaven's sake, anything but that!' he cried. 'I, a scholar? Never!'

I was taken aback.

'A scholar,' he explained, 'is a beast of burden—the noblest beast of burden, I grant, but a beast of burden nevertheless, a donkey. Look at your great Professor R., more meek, more long-suffering, and more obstinate than any donkey, the very quintessence of donkeyism. A yogi told me once that according to the theory of transmigration, a donkey that has not pestered too many females is reborn a scholar. A scholar, groaning under the weight of other people's thoughts—there is no fire in his soul; he is cold to the touch. You know, I was fortunate. I never went to school.'

Sanki was silent for a moment, or rather, he hummed to himself. Then: 'The terrible thing is that, having transmigrated, they have lost even the capacity for pestering females.'

Usually my part in these conversations was simply mute admiration, but one day I said, 'You know, you have a marvellous gift, why don't you make use of it? Why don't you write something really serious, something to drown the cackle of this modern poetry?'

'I am not a modest man, and I agree with whatever you say,' he said. 'And the fact is, I don't like modern poetry myself. It's so easily done. Write a page of prose, cut it down the middle, and you have two pages of poetry. Besides, it's so hard and fierce. I throw a handful of those lines into the hollow of my soul, and they fall like clattering marbles on a stone floor. They should burst like little bombs, but softly, filling your being with a glowing vapour. That is what poetry should do, that is its only

purpose—filling the hollow in man. But, speaking seri-
ously, I am contemplating a big poem. It will be my
magnum opus. The subject will be, *The Woman Who Was
Twenty Months Pregnant.*' Then he carelessly went
away, without even wishing me a good-by.

2

One day I was reading in the public library when I saw him
come in. He stood in a corner with an undecided air, biting
his nails. I went up to him. His face lit up when he saw
me. 'Ah, how lucky!' he said. 'Look, you have to do some
work for me.'

'Work?' I said. 'What is it?'

Sanki whispered like a conspirator. 'I have solved
the riddle of all history and civilization. What I need is a
short historical survey of every country in the world and
what its national animal is.'

I looked puzzled.

'Yes, you'll have to do it,' he said. 'No hurry,
whenever you have the time. Let's go get a cup of tea, this
place is horribly gloomy. It's more depressing than a
cemetery. Souls of poets dead and gone, leather-bound
and dusty souls. They should have destroyed their works
before they died . . . Wait! Is Hafiz in here?'

'Yes.'

'Where?'

'Oh, over there somewhere.' I waved vaguely.

'I shall break in tonight and get him out. Good
Lord! The open-air drunkard of Shiraz must be gasping
in this place.'

14

Over tea, he told me of his discovery. 'It is the destiny of every nation to strive to become its national animal. Now, take the case of India. National animal, the cow. Have you ever seen anything more philosophical and nonviolent? No, obviously not. The pursuit of our five thousand years of civilization has been nothing less than to become cows. Vedanta is the finest flower of our culture, and it is nothing but bovine contemplation. Take the Arabs. Their national animal is the camel. Have you heard the rich, throaty, bubbling cry of a camel? The Arabic language was born out of that. You don't dispute it, do you? Just listen to an Arab speak and you'll know how right I am. And the dream and ambition of every Arab has been to reach a perfection in language to match the camel. You must have heard of those incredible tales, how an average Arab can keep up a dialogue in verse for hours, how orators never repeat the same word for a whole year. The world has not known a people more language-proud than that. And what does it come to in the end? To be a camel, that's what.'

I was dumbfounded.

'Think of Greece,' Sanki went on. 'In their slave-ridden society, 'man' was the national animal, and wasn't the dream of their philosophy to perfect this animal?'

'What about England?' I said. 'I think their national animal is the lion.'

'What, the lion!' he cried in bewilderment. 'How like the British! They never saw a lion until a few centuries back. You know, England is a tiny island with plenty of ocean around it. So their national animal should come from the sea—the dolphin, for instance . . . no, not the dolphin, the shark. Yes, it's the shark, and every

Englishman knows it but won't confess it. How else can you explain England's great seafaring tradition, her imperialism and preying on others?'

'Tell me, what about America? They don't seem to have one.'

'That's easy. The national animal of America is the machine; and people who have been there tell me that American civilization follows with ruthless persistence the course of making men into automatons. The movements of the machine have passed into the movements of men. You can see the pistons move, the wheels go round. It's amazing, it's tragic, but there is no escape from destiny.'

'And the lion?'

'Oh, yes. The lion is the international animal. Every civilization wants to become the lion in the end. That explains wars, and also why the English gave it British citizenship—those people have a knack of calling everything English that they like best.'

He had been drinking tea and smoking all this while in nervous excitement, as if trying to find a kind of equilibrium. The amount of tea and tobacco he used to consume in those days astonished me. When he had finished talking, I said, 'A fascinating idea, Sanki, but I'm afraid it won't stand the test of logic.'

He flared up. 'What do I care for logic? Logic is the biggest lie of all history! Bah! They should have put Aristotle to death for misleading the world with his syllogism, instead of that innocent prattler, Socrates. No man has climbed to a big thought on the ladder of logic. All two-legged animals are men. Abdul is a two-legged animal. Therefore Abdul is a man. How tragically pathetic! Even the village barber knows that Abdul is a man. Logic pretends to prove things which are obvious.'

And then he left—abruptly, as was his habit.

3

I did not see Sanki again for many months, but then one evening I caught sight of him in the pit of a cinema hall. He was holding an earthenware cup in each hand and sipping tea out of them in turn. He looked more shabby and dishevelled than ever. After the film I caught up with him.

'You here?' I said, with surprise evident in my voice.

'Yes, I like this film. I have seen it seventy-three times. That surprises you?'

'Yes,' I admitted, 'it does.'

'I thought it would. But has it ever occurred to you that the evening is a terrible time for a lonely and sensitive man? Up to thirty he can fool himself with silly entertainments—after that the game is up. The thought of my evenings makes me shudder; they wait for me like a dragon. I don't know what ugly face of my soul I see between six and ten. I don't understand it—I run like a hunted animal and usually I cannot escape. But whenever I do manage to find an escape, like this film, I cling hard to it, until that escape is no longer an escape.'

We went into a tea shop and sat at a corner table. 'It's a pity,' he said meditatively. 'No one has given any thought to this, no one has tried to find a remedy. There seems to be only one—drink. But I don't like it. Too fiery,

17

and besides, it gives me violent convulsions of the nerves. I am sure there must be some remedy, something soothing, something like soft mist to fill the chasm of the soul between six and ten.'

We sat talking for a long time that night. Sanki was full of his loneliness and kept on complaining. 'I wish I had a buffalo's hide and brains. The more you understand, the more miserable you are. I can feel my brain cells burning up, and sometimes the light hurts my eyes. And my most beautiful dreams, one by one they have burned to ash under my gaze, just because of the gaze. How I envy the stupid with half-shut eyes! And then this condemnation to eternal solitude, yes, so lonely and essentially separate. In my weariness I try to attach myself to people. I throw myself against the net of humanity and try to be caught in it like a flying-fox, but every time I fall to the ground. I carry the devil about in me. I seem to be in search of something, but I do not know what it is. It sounds so mad. It has ruined my life and the restlessness is killing me.'

His eyes looked inexpressibly sad, and he was miles and miles inside himself. I suppose he did not even know that I was sitting there.

'I know I belong nowhere and to no one,' he went on. 'Even the wish for a collar and chain falls away, and again the mad quest. Last night I took a dangerous step forward. When I am at grips with higher things, thoughts lose their solidity and outline—they resemble vague forms moving in the minds of animals, like clouds at dusk; and then the roar of night. That is the end. In higher thought the will does not function at all, the cloud-forms come and go of their own will, and one is helpless like a sleeper struggling in his dream. Last night, it did not end in chaos. I managed an almost fatal step forward. I saw God! I walked off the edge of space and was face to face with eternity. It frightened me like a vast night. You know, God is a king cobra. I didn't see, but I heard him. Hiss, hiss—the black lightning of his forked tongue. Terror held me motionless. And then the water lapped in the dark. I don't know which is God, the hissing cobra or the lapping water. Maybe both. But both are terrible. I woke up shaking with sobs. Then I lit the lamp and sat in a strange mood of sad exultation. I could have explained to you what is good and what is evil. I had the secret in the palm of my hand. I could have pulled out the black thread that holds the beads of the stars together. But then dawn came, like a weeping woman, and I fell asleep with a cold ache in my shoulder blades.'

Absently, he lit a cigarette, and both of us sat in silence. There was a hunted look in his eyes. We heard the familiar sounds of a restaurant closing for the night—chairs being piled on tables, a man cursing somewhere in the back. We rose and stepped out into the cool night. I said something, but he didn't hear me. Then I hailed a rickshaw and offered to drop him at his place. He said no, and wandered off. He lived only for a year after that. He died at the age of thirty-one.

When I heard the news of his death, I rushed to his room. He was lying in a corner, leaner than a ghost at cockcrow. He had a cruel grin on his face, and his very sharp features looked sharper than ever. The room was filthy—a few rags on the floor, a bed which apparently hadn't been slept in for a long time. A torn volume of the poems of Hafiz lay by the side of the corpse. On the floor were innumerable scraps of paper with verses scribbled on them, some partly burned and twisted. Some day, when I have money, I shall bring out a collection of my friend's poems. I put a copy of the poems of Hafiz in his grave, for, I thought, it would do his soul good; there was no one who loved and knew Hafiz better than he did.

The naked parrot lives with me now. Every evening it sets up a squawking, and I give it a pellet of opium which quiets it down. Then it sits in its corner, dreaming—I do not know what.

TIME TO GO

Kashi never paid the coffee bill. It was always one of us who had to do it. Normally we did not mind, but there were days when we could not help a feeling of resentment. On such occasions, although we said nothing, he saw what was passing through our minds and, in order to pacify us, would say, 'I am sorry I can't pay.' We knew he couldn't—he could hardly make both ends meet—but at the same time we thought he wouldn't even if he could. And, as if replying to our unuttered thoughts, he would say, 'No, I don't think I would pay even if I had the money. You would think it was your little moral pressure made me do so.'

It was this unnecessary offensiveness in his nature that alienated most of his friends from him, turning some into bitter enemies. But he did not care. He grew reckless when an idea excited him and he began to talk. He even forgot that the idea would sometimes be sitting across the table in the shape of a friend standing him the coffee, as he went on beautifully and relentlessly with the analysis. His mind was like a powerful machine and the words came in rapid succession. How low, mean and utterly despicable men were! How base in their motives! If they stood you a cup of coffee, they wanted lies and flattery in return. Sometimes it ended in a scuffle and foul language and the manager would come running and everyone would gather around us. But the sensible ones avoided making a scene. They would get up in a rage and leave, call him a swine when out of the range of his hearing, and vow never to mix with him again.

In the end only three of us were left with him—Vikram, Anand and myself. It was not that he spared us. That would have been against his nature. But we learnt to keep out of the way of his mind. Besides, we liked our names being linked with his—the apostles of a denouncing prophet. And finally, we thought that we too were cynics like him—snakes, and the bite of one snake does not kill another.

Kashi lived in a small room in the Civil Lines surrounded by books and chaos. He read voraciously but unmethodically, and it was always physics, mathematics, philosophy and such hard going for which we had no use. What we read he called literary garbage. He had been a brilliant student at the University, and his professors and friends had thought that he would be a great name one day. But when I returned from the Burmah front, where I had been a war journalist for a year, I found that he had left the University without obtaining a degree. To read, he said. To read and rot.

We usually spent our evenings at the coffee-house. I got off work at five o'clock. I would bathe and change and herd Vikram and Anand to Kashi's room, where we would stop a while and then the four of us would push on to the coffee-house. We affected a corner table and would settle down there for the evening—smoking, sipping coffee, arguing and disputing. It was a noisy and cheerful place, full of smoke, laughter, undergraduates and young lawyers.

One reason why Kashi approved of the coffee-house was that women did not go there. They inhibit you by their presence, he said of them. They constipate your laughter. He would even give a scientific explanation: man had one magnetic field, woman another, each different from and contradicting the other. It could be most easily demonstrated. Place iron filings upon a sheet of glass and put a human couple underneath and ask them to behave, and there will be tension in the iron filings. Men and women are best apart. A man-and-woman civilization was bound to be a neurotic civilization because of the constant strain of each other's presence. And so on, the whole evening. He would take up culture, morality, love, truth and maintain that they were all dirty glass screens fashioned by men so that they could hide behind them. One by one he took them up and smashed them with a hammer, so to say. We enjoyed it as the splinters flew. Every evening a philosophy, a sacred principle or a time-honoured practice went by the board.

At ten o'clock the coffee-house would close and we would emerge into the cool, fresh air outside after the overheated atmosphere of the room. Sauntering to the betel-seller's and chewing *pan*, we would part for the evening, immensely satisfied. Kashi's dark words reverberated in our minds, and the sharp jagged ideas kept returning. If by any chance he had lashed out against one of us, we had our revenge by demolishing him *in absentia*.

One evening, much later than usual, because I had been detained at the office, we called on him. I did not find Vikram at home, so there were just the two of us, Anand and myself. We reached his room and I pushed the door open. Probably he had heard us come, for when we entered we saw him lying on his battered leather sofa, kicking his heels in the air like a child and making little sounds of glee. We knew it was one of his excitable days.

'Angels and minister of grace, defend us!' Anand cried good-humouredly.

Kashi sat up.

'What in the name of heaven is this madness?' I said.

'It is not madness. It is happiness,' he stated.

'What is the great occasion?' I said.

'Have you read this?' he asked me, pushing a folded newspaper towards me.

'No,' I said, glancing at the print, 'is it about Hiroshima?'

'Well read it. After the vulgar details of death and destruction that one atom bomb can cause, there is a bit about a chain-reaction setting in.'

I did not get the drift of his meaning, so I drew my eyebrows together in inquiry. 'Chain-reaction!' he said impatiently. 'Don't you follow?' His voice rose in excitement as he continued. 'One atom exploding and lighting up another, and so on and on until the earth also blows up—like a squib, reduced to a flash of radiation and absorbed in space.'

Suddenly his voice fell and he said, 'But the chances are meagre, one in a million or a hundred million! But if they drop a thousand bombs the chances will be much brighter.' Once again his voice rose. 'The best thing about chance is that the lucky one may be the first one.'

'What is there to be so happy about in this?' I asked, 'it's silly and depressing.' The edge in my voice provoked him.

'Good heavens, man!' he shouted, throwing up his arms. 'Are you in your senses? Imagine what a stupendous ending it will be to our tame drama! An exit on a heroic scale! We shall give a jolt to the universe. Our insignificant home in space giving a sharp jolt to the infinite universe—imagine! Is that nothing? Fountains, cascades and arches of flame will whistle through space like the furies. The dust we shall raise will reach the very confines of space. And you find it depressing? For countless aeons the stars have travelled wearily, their eyes tired of the emptiness of desert space, hungering for something to happen, for up there things rarely happen. What have they seen but fire-flies in the forest of the night? We shall give them a splendid spectacle. The flash will go like a spear through every stellar eye. And the mighty plume of smoke will rise and rise till it has enmeshed the stars. And you find no cause for jubilation? Imagine the immense possibilities! Suppose we started a chain-reaction up there! All the crackers of heaven will explode, space will be twisted and the ever-flowing river of time will dry up.'

He was almost panting with excitement, and now he tried to hold himself back. The shadow of a smile passed over his face, and he said in a flat voice, 'Besides, we shall have blackened the face of the sun. The bright face blackened! And by the time he wipes the soot off and looks again the earth will have gone, and where it was would be a hole, a cavity in space. I find the situation positively amusing. Don't you?' Both of us smiled as he pretended to look into space for the vanished earth with a comic screw of his eye. Then with a theatrical gesture he said, 'Gentlemen, you are my guests tonight! The occasion calls for celebrations: we shall drink today, coffee will be too tame.'

We never objected to a celebration. Besides, it was almost ten o'clock and the coffee-house would soon be closing, so we trooped out and went to Rama's bar with him. It was a little place with a bare polished floor, frosted-glass doors and subdued lights; no noise and very little smoke. And not too many people either. When we reached it there were only three men sitting at the farthest table and drinking in melancholy silence. Alcohol never produces in us the abandon it is supposed to. The reason probably is that we approach it in a spirit of suspicion. We might forget everything but we never forget that we are drinking.

Kashi ordered the drinks. When the waiter brought them and put them on the table, he raised his glass and said, 'To the imminent doom of our dear planet!' We said, 'Amen!' We lit our cigarettes, sipped the whisky and sank into a relaxed silence.

Anand was the first to speak. 'Suppose we started the atomic game and your fireworks didn't come off, we'd look a set of fools, wouldn't we?'

'Probably we would,' he replied, 'more in keeping with our rotten luck. Still there will be some consolation. Mankind will at least be effaced. We can't bear so much hurt. Once it starts it will be terrible. The dead everywhere, rotting and stinking! And the living, worse for them. Millions blinded! And no one to hold their hands even! Creeping, crawling and praying for death! And the showers of radioactive ash! It won't be the ash of a great repentance. It will be too late for that as the radiation pricks every nerve and fibre of the body. And the next generation will be done for too, the unborn, guiltless generation, as the radiation plays havoc with the genes and the chromosomes. We shall put a burning cactus into every mother's womb.'

He tossed off the last mouthful of whisky that was in his glass, and asked the waiter to bring us another round of drinks. I looked at him as he lit his cigarette. His face was tense, the skin over his cheekbones stretching white. His red hair was untidy as usual, and in his green Kashmiri eyes a spark was dancing. He had a habit of sometimes pulling up his eyebrows that gave his eyes a Mongolian tilt of cruelty.

'And then,' he continued, 'humanity, with its body broken, will lie down to die. Millions of years ago mighty lizards ruled the earth, so huge that the earth shook at their tread, and there were nightmare birds with teeth like a double saw and the shrieks of their victims filled the air. Then doom struck. Came a drought and a mighty famine. The lizards began to die and the great birds flopped to the ground. They rested their dying heads on the parched soil and their big eyes rolled in perplexity as to what was happening—what was happening to the lords of the earth! For thousands of years their bones bleached in the sun. . . '

He did not stop for an hour. What with the liquor and his incessant talk my mind was in a whirl. I thought a breath of fresh air would do me good. So I got up and went outside. The night was cool, the roads deserted. A

27

couple of rickshaws stood at the roadside. There was a pendent light over the crossing and moths were circling around it. On either side of the road for some distance stood tamarind trees, overarching the road and mixing their branches. They formed a city for the birds. As twilight fell they came in flocks and kept up an uneasy stir in the trees till the gloom deepened and the peace of the night began. I shook my head to clear the fog that was in it. A crow fluttered and cawed. I stood under a tree, made water, and returned.

The men at the other table had risen to go. Our company was quiet. Anand was resting his head on the table, his eyes closed and his listless fingers circling his glass. We used to tell him that his drinking was like the going out of an oil lamp. One drink did not do much harm, two made him quiet and he smiled stupidly at everything, three made him half shut his eyes and slowed his responses, and the fourth extinguished him. Kashi's brow was knit in a frown. He was deep in thought, and was smoking.

'Let's have another,' he said, as I dropped into my chair.

'Don't you think we have had enough?' I suggested.

'Let this be the last.'

'All right.'

For ten or fifteen minutes we sat in silence, taking an occasional sip.

'I think there is an inevitability about our doom,' he said.

'Oh, no. We'd come through all right,' I said.

'But do we want to? I think we have had enough of this damned business of living and would like to go.'

'You mean we'll kill ourselves, race suicide? No, I don't believe it.'

'Why not? If one man can do it, why not the race?'

'Bad enough in one, but in a race,' I shook my head. 'You forget self-preservation.'

'Self-preservation,' he repeated the word slowly, 'how long do you want it? The sensible get over it soon enough and wish for death. Haven't you heard that death gives you the moment of truth? And once you have seen the truth, you don't want to live any more.'

'I don't believe it.'

'Don't! I'm not asking you to believe it. What you want is something soft and sweet. That is what all hunger for, soft and sweet lies.'

'No, it's not that all. It's your wanting to wallow in it . . .'

He flushed and his eyes sparkled. 'No, I hate it all," he cried. 'What is there to wallow in? I hate myself. I hate you and I hate all the lies that we have built up.'

'Whatever you say,' I said calmly, 'I don't believe we shall commit suicide. We shall never do such a cowardly thing.'

He gave a gasp. 'Cowardly!' he exclaimed, 'you are drunk. This will be the most heroic act we shall have done. We shall face annihilation by our own choice. Do you realize the tremendous implications, and therefore the great sacrifice?'

'No,' I said hopelessly.

'A species grows out of itself only when faced with annihilation. Nothing short of it brings forth the supreme effort. Other dangers ring a bell only in the mind, annihilation sounds the alarm in every cell of the body and the whole animal heaves and comes out on a different plane. Sometimes it doesn't. But this threat is its only chance.'

'War as an aid to evolution?' I asked.

'Oh, no!' he sighed. 'War is a vulgarity that does no good to life or death. It only satisfies our instinct to humiliate the other fellow. I don't believe in war, but I believe in annihilation with which nature has faced species from time to time. The *Homo sapiens* have reached a stage where nature cannot threaten them in that way. So isn't it heroic to create the threat for ourselves?'

'There is some satisfaction in that,' I said. 'We shall be dying, it seems, for a cause.'

'Nonsense!' he said. 'Who has ever died for a cause? They have all died for themselves, to a man.'

'All right,' I said. 'Have it your own way. But let us rejoice in the new species we shall be creating.'

'Why should I? Who will they be to me? They'll look down upon us. We shall be the dunghill on which the fine flower sprang. Instead you join with me in my prayer that our planet may be blown up.'

He put down his glass with a clatter that made Anand wake up. Sitting up with an effort, he looked at us with half-open, bleary eyes. Kashi raised his hands in prayer and said, 'O, the Almighty Nothingness, in which knots of matter have formed like disease cysts, and which will dissolve in time into pure nothingness. O, the Eternal Darkness, on which have appeared pimples of light, and which will vanish into pure darkness again! O, the Everlasting Silence, temporarily broken by songs and laments, hear the prayer of this humble devotee of yours and blow up this planet and as many more as you conveniently can! O, the Almighty, Silent, Dark Nothingness, with me join two miserable sinners, and one of them is so drunk that he cannot even lift up his hands. Amen!'

'Amen,' I said.

In a few minutes the waiter came along and said it was midnight and time to close. 'Time to go,' I said, and helped Anand to his feet. We opened the door and staggered out. From a distance, when we had left the roof of trees behind, we saw the bar lights go out. Kashi stood in the middle of the road, and pointing to the sky said, 'See that blackboard? All that writing will be wiped off.' Then making a wild gesture with his hand he shouted with the fury of a maniac, 'Turn out the stellar lights. It's time to go!'

For an hour or so Hamid had been trying to read. An open book lay on the table before him. He sat erect and read: 'The same with the boys. First and foremost establish a rule over them, a proud, harsh, manly rule. Make them know . . .' then the words lost all their meaning, ceased to register on the mind. It was the late February air that was making him so drowsy. He had read that page he did not remember how many times and was still reading it at the end of an hour. He shook himself, got up and walked to the window.

The college buildings seemed to be sleeping in the Sunday quiet. The huge tamarind trees looked like shaggy monsters waiting to awaken some day. Under them a narrow gravelled road went zigzagging in the direction of the city. Dreamily Hamid contemplated the view, and suddenly discovered that he had been thinking of the girl in the prostitutes' quarter whom he had visited last month. Now he frankly gave himself up to thinking about her. He had had a lot of fun with her. She was young and good-looking—a healthy animal, probably a village girl. She was certainly new to the trade—the way she kept averting her face and resisting him. A feeling of voluptuousness came over him, a desire to press something. Moving from the window, he strolled to the mirror, and stood before it looking at his reflection. He had not shaved for two days and his chin was stubbly. He drew the back of his hand over the rough surface and smiled in response to some pleasant thought.

It was past eleven that night when he bribed the hall-porter, the iron gate creaked on its hinges and he escaped furtively into the night. Outside it was cool and fresh and a breeze rustled the leaves of the trees which were ominously silhouetted in the dark. The sky was gemmed with stars. There was no one about. A bus passed him carrying only three passengers. Shortly, he passed Madhu's corner. The blind beggar was still there keeping up with harsh monotony the repetition of the name of God. He seemed an untiring and articulate woodpecker, uttering the same cry hour after hour—*Hari Ram, Hari Ram, Hari Ram.* . . . In the stillness the sound pursued him a long distance and irritated him. But soon he was out of its reach.

Here and there lights shone in some windows, otherwise the place was asleep. He passed the railway overbridge and entered the old part of the city. There was much more light here, and some shops were still open, mostly sweetmeat-and-milk shops and betel shops, where people sat on wooden benches drinking milk out of earthenware cups or stood chewing *pan* or smoking cigarettes and looking at themselves in the huge mirrors that decorated the betel shops. He went on. Street *ekkas* ambled past him. A rickshaw pulled up at his side, but he did not take it. He was in no hurry and preferred to walk. He reached the clock-tower which stood in the congested heart of the city. Stray cattle had herded under its shadow to pass the night. He looked at the motionless white heaps, and taking a careful look around dove into a side-alley.

A fetid smell from the open drains greeted him, and a flower-seller hurried towards him to sell him a flower-chain. He was a young man, an emaciated dandy in a muslin *kurta* and green silk *tahband,* who had sacrificed his youth to the traders of love who lived here. Long, white jasmine chains hung from his arm. Hamid did not buy one, and the sharp smell of jasmine irritated him. There was little and broken light in the long alley, and some corners were completely dark. Here too business for the day had concluded, and those customers who had stayed on preferred the lights out. In a few low balconies some women still sat under the glare of electric lights, waiting. He looked up at them, at the overpainted faces and the inviting, entreating eyes. A sudden disgust filled him and he felt as if a shower of ashes had fallen over him. In his mind awoke the reek of sweet oils, cheap scents and stale perspiration. The underclothing had always been frowzy.

The occasional lights made sharp outlines in the dim alley. He passed on till he reached a door, where he knocked. An old woman opened the door.

'Is Vimla free?' he asked.

'Yes,' said the woman.

'I'll come in,' he said, stepping in. 'It'll be for the whole night.'

'All right. I'll go and tell her. We had finished for the night.'

34

She opened another door and disappeared. He did not sit. There was a suffocating smell in the room. The old woman's sheetless bed was in a corner. The quilt was faded and horribly stained, and the pillow was shiny with layers of dirt and oil. She had spat freely and an area of six inches on the floor was messy with sputum in which showed yellow blobs of phlegm. He lit a cigarette to disinfect his nostrils and looked at the ceiling. It was so low he could have touched it with his hand if he were a little taller.

The woman returned. He counted out twenty rupees, and as he was going in she asked him for a cigarette. He gave her one.

The other room was much cleaner. Vimla was sitting on the side of her bed with her bare feet dangling. She had been lying in bed and had sat up to receive her customer.

'Oh, it's you!' she said, smiling.

'So you remember me?' he said.

'Why, of course, you were among my first customers.'

'Was I?'

'Yes,' she said, and smiled again.

Then she grew serious as if some reflection held her mind, and he watched her. She was looking far more beautiful and sure of herself than before. Last time, careless wisps of hair had strayed about her face and her eyes had a frightened look. She had seemed lost. Now her hair was tastefully braided, a trifle too oily he thought, and lamp-black darkened her eyes and tailed out at the corners. He did not like her.

'Shall we?' she said, breaking the silence and meaning to undress. She got up and had a drink of water from an earthenware pitcher that stood in the corner. A crumbled rose fell out of her hair. She pushed it under the bed with her foot.

Half an hour later she said in the dark, 'What do you do?'

'I read, I'm a student,' he said. He was blaming himself for paying for the whole night. There was no more desire left in him and he wished he could go away and sleep in the freedom of his own bed.

'Do you belong here?' she asked.

'No.'

'You have come here to read?'

'Yes.'

'How long have you been here?'

'Three years. One more and I'll be gone.'

'I've been here two months,' she said.

'I know,' he said. 'Wasn't I among your first customers?'

'Oh!' she said.

A breath of cold air swept in at the window and she, her head on his reluctant arm, shivered. 'We came to the Kumbh Fair, my parents and I,' she said hesitatingly.

'And you stayed on?' he said ironically.

'Yes, I stayed on,' she said. 'My parents were killed in the big crush.'

'I'm sorry,' he said, 'I didn't mean to be a brute.'

'I don't know whether they died or not, but I never saw them again. A hundred died that day,' she said and added meditatively, 'I hope they are dead.'

He felt intrigued. Her last words were so toneless and calm that he did not know what to make of them. He heard her slow breathing.

'Why did so many people have to die? They had come to pray,' she said.

'I'm sure I don't know. Maybe prayer doesn't make any difference,' he said.

'Did you go there that day?'

'No, I didn't, but I read about it,' he said. 'The newspapers carried everything.'

The Kumbh was a bathing festival, and the third of January was the biggest bathing day. The Ganga, flowing from the foot of Vishnu and through Shiva's hair tumbles out of the Himalayas into the plains of Northern India, and touching scores of cities and towns and edging thousands of villages, joins the Jamuna at Prayag in its course to the sea. Here at the confluence of these two great rivers another joins them, Saraswati, an invisible stream cascading from heaven, and makes Prayag one of the most holy places in the land. The Kumbh falls every twelve years. Millions of people come to Prayag from every corner of India on this occasion, and have done so for over three thousand years, eager for a dip in the holy waters that would rid them of their sins and ensure their salvation.

Five million people converged on Prayag that year, making the assembly probably the greatest concourse of humanity in known history. Fifty special trains arrived every day; aeroplanes roared in the sky all time of the day and night and the high roads were alive with every type of vehicle ranging from the motor car to the bullock cart. Even then the vast majority of people had to come on foot. Along the railway tracks on both sides there were unbroken lines of people for a hundred miles. These men and women mostly tramped in silence, carrying heavy bundles strapped to their backs or slung on bamboo-sticks across their shoulders. Sometimes to beguile the weary hours they chanted holy songs. And all the time the overloaded trains thundered past them with people crowded on footboards and hanging onto the handrails, sitting astride on buffers, and precariously perched on the roofs of the carriages by the hundred.

At Prayag the river front for twelve miles had become a *caravansarai*. If you ascended a high embankment you saw a new town spread out like a map before you. The contracted river wound eastward through thousands of thatched huts that covered the white sands. At nightfall the design of the sprawling town flashed into view as electric lights went on and oil lamps were lit. Thousands of fires flickered in the dark and awakened mysterious feelings. Brahma may or may not be there, but there certainly was something in the air.

'A thin rain fell the whole night,' she said. 'We could not afford a shelter. The *sadhus* were overcharging so much, and we had but little money. My mother called them godless people, but my father told her not to complain; they had come to pray and not to grumble. So the rain beat on us and the wind was very cold. We shivered and prayed, and my father said that God was kind and he prayed that he might die there, for the fortunate who die there go straight to heaven.

'The bathing started much before dawn. In the morning the sky cleared and a bright sun came out. We had a dip in the river and were feeling very happy. I saw the hair that had been shaved off people's heads. I had never seen so much hair. A whole field was covered with it and it was removed by the boatful.

'As the morning wore on the crowd grew thicker and thicker, jostling and elbowing and pressing. We stood on one side and waited for the holy men to give their *darshan*. At last they came, riding on elephants and surrounded by naked *sadhus* brandishing tridents. The people in front formed a wall and the procession passed at a leisurely pace. The pressure from behind increased as more and more people poured down the embankment to have a closer view of the holy men. Then came a strong wave from behind that flattened the wall in front. Those who fell could not get up and were trampled to death. Such cries filled the air! People went mad, I think. They shouted and pushed and fell and walked on one another. Some got under the elephants' feet. I cried and could not find my parents. I saw a dead child and her eyes were lying out, and there was an old man, his belly had burst and people's heels went into it, and there were dead women, and some with child too. Oh, it was horrible! I was ready to faint, but I knew that falling was certain death, so I clung to those next to me.

'Is it true that a hundred died that day? More! Well, the situation eased off after a bit. In my helplessness, and blind with tears, I asked people if they had seen my parents, an old man and an old woman. Some did not answer, some said no. Then a man held me by the hand and said: "Sister, there are some wounded lying on that side, come and look there." He gripped my hand and I followed and we went through the crowd. I did not know what was happening around me and I walked as if in a dream. He took me into a hut, and suddenly turning round put his hand across my mouth. I was too dazed to realize what he was doing. He gagged me and tying my hands behind my back pushed me hard into a corner. I fell and struck my head on a stool. He muttered a few threats and said he would kill me if I stirred or tried to escape. I lay there in pain and fear, crying the whole day and far into the night. I knew I would never see my parents again. I was faint with hunger and crying, and weakness brought on sleep.' She fetched a sigh and added, 'He brought me here, and the rest of the story you know.'

'Why don't you do something about it?' Hamid spoke with indignation.

'What can I do? Besides, what am I good for now?' she said.

'Oh, that's nonsense. Where's your home?' he asked.

'In Raipur. It's a village eighty miles from here. We walked.' He thought in silence, and she continued, 'I never dreamed I would ever lead such a life. But I suppose it was my fate.'

'No, it's nobody's fate to lead such a life,' he said angrily. 'Look, why don't you get out of this, go home and live your own life instead of making money for this swine?'

She did not answer. He thought the man (who turned out to be the old woman's son) must have threatened to kill her if she tried to run away. How could he help her? Two thousand women between the ages of fifteen and twenty-five were reported missing during the fair. This was where they went. The police knew that interstate gangs of kidnappers were active, and they were vigilant, yet . . .

'I dreamed of home only once in all this time,' she said, talking again. 'That night I had my first client. I knew he was coming and I cried my eyes out. They made me up. My head was splitting with ache. And then he came, a middle-aged man. He was stout and had grey hairs on his temples.' She stopped as if to see him again in her mind, and said, 'He was a kind man. He stayed for two hours. He must have been drunk. He held my chin and turned my face and viewed me from arm's length and said I was a *devi*. He seemed a nice man. When he left I was tired and fell asleep and I dreamed that I was home. My father was working in the fields and I took his mid-day meal to him. There was moist earth sticking to his hands. He was very happy to see me and pressed me to him and said, "Daughter, you have come! We looked for you everywhere, where did you go?" And I burst out crying, and clung to him and said, "Why did you leave me like that?" I must have cried in my sleep, for when I woke up my pillow was wet, and the old woman sitting by my bed was crying too. She is not a bad person. She is always very kind to me.'

'Of course, she'd be kind to you,' Hamid said angrily. 'You go on making money for them and they'll be kind to you. Kindness doesn't cost anything.'

'No, it's not that,' she said.

Hamid's mind was in a turmoil when he emerged from there and he thought furiously as he walked home. It hadn't grown light yet but he could sense the morning air. There was not a soul abroad. Even the human woodpecker Madhu was not at his station to break the stillness with the senseless repetition of the name of God. He reached his room and from time to time a vast emptiness revolved in his mind. He tried to sleep but could not.

At nine in the morning he returned to his previous

night's rendezvous with a police inspector. They knocked at the door and were met by a thin, long-haired man. Knowing who they were and the purpose of their visit he asked them to come in. The old woman was in panic when she learnt why they had come. She rushed into Vimla's room saying that she would wake her up.

Vimla joined them in a few minutes. Her face was puffy and her eyes were heavy with sleep. Hamid smiled to her. But she did not return the smile. A flush came to her face as the questioning proceeded. He could not believe his ears when he heard her tell the police officer that she had come of her own accord and the question of her going back did not arise at all.

'But you told me last night . . .' Hamid began, when she cut in sharply.

'Never mind what I told you last night.' There was a hostile glitter in her eyes as she looked at him.

'But try to understand, I want to help you,' he replied.

'No one helps a prostitute. She has to help herself.' She spoke bitterly in a tone that said much more than the words. It sounded like an accusation, not of him—he seemed too small for that—but of something much bigger. He was quiet.

As there was nothing more to be said or done after that, they left. Outside the older man said, 'You are a student. Why should you get mixed up with such women?'

'I wanted to help her go home', he said.

'But she couldn't go home after what has happened,' the older man said.

'Why not? It's not her fault.'

'Who'll bother about that? She has been in the

profession, and that's all that matters. By force or choice that's immaterial. Her reputation would follow her to the village. The accused man will see to it that it reaches there. What do you think her life would be like after that? The villagers would make it impossible for her to live there. Not only for her but for her parents too. No matter where she goes people would be cruel to her once they know her secret,' the older man explained.

Hamid remembered her calling the old woman and some of the customers kind. Hers was a dirty, heartless world, he thought, but there was an occasional tear shed in it for her, and it was that which was holding her to it.

Mehdi Hasan, professor of philosophy, was dying of brain cancer. He could not be operated upon, for the removal of the malignant tumour would involve the destruction of too much brain-tissue. The news, when the doctor told him, hit him, as they say, like a truck, knocking the vehicle of his life off the highway into a ditch. His reason, on which he had relied heavily all his life, was the first casualty. How could an occasional headache and a stiff neck add up to death? How can one and one make infinity? His emotions fared no better. Fear heaved and sloshed in his whole being with a force that threatened to split the container.

But time is a healer, or at least a deadener. Within a few weeks he had calmed down and his faculties regained a measure of self-control and resumed, at least partly, their ordinary functioning. For example, his reason, though still unable to join a minor cause to a major effect with the straight line of logic, managed to draw the crooked line of paradox between his harmless symptoms and catastrophic diagnosis. His emotional tumult also subsided to a dull quiescence. He became sadly reconciled to the fact that the colourful, noisy show of life would go on merrily but shortly he would no longer be a part of it.

However, the semblance of repose that his resignation had brought him did not last long. It began to be threatened by an image. He would be sitting by himself in a headache-free period or lying awake at night, when an image would appear before his mental vision, the image of a dark wall. He could see himself standing before it, his progress and view completely cut off. He was an intelligent as well as a highly educated man. So he knew immediately what the wall stood for. It was his mind's way of telling him in concrete terms that he had reached the end of his street. Every man's life is a dead-end street, and one day he reaches the point after which there is nowhere else to go. He must accept this finality. Mehdi had done exactly that.

But his imagination would not go along with him. It created difficulties for him. It said: 'This is a wall. A wall has two sides. There must be something on the other side.' Mehdi thought that in his weakened state old religious superstitions that he had successfully driven off were beginning to return. He had been sure—the training of a life-time had taught him so—that death is extinction, a total annihilation. He remembered stepping on insects, sometimes accidentally, sometimes deliberately. That was death—being rubbed out of existence. But his imagination would not listen. Unreasonably it kept on repeating its demand for the perspective on the other side. What made Mehdi uneasy in the beginning and tense and frustrated later on was the easy erosion of his reasoned conviction and the increasing presence of the illusion of the other side. He could not get the thought out of his mind. His devout Muslim friends tried to come to his aid. They said they knew what was on the other side. First of all there was God. Then there were his angels, and his devils. And that he would be met by an angel in the grave who would ask him for an account of his life. Mehdi, who had been brought up in a Muslim household, was familiar with these beliefs. But they were fictions for him that did not carry conviction. They did not touch his imagination, which stood there obstinately before the dark wall, trying to pierce it with its eyes. What was he to do? He started to fear his headache-free periods. The headache was a pain that he could understand, but the pain of the imagination, the heavy anxiety, the constant but futile spinning of the mind drove him to utter exhaustion, yet made no sense.

He devised a distraction for his mind, which went as follows: 'Keep the mind steadily looking at the truth of your death. Tie it firmly to the fact so that it does not stray into the illusion. The wall is not really a wall but a concrete block without end. There is no other side.'

It was this principle that he was practising on that October afternoon when the snake-charmer turned up at his door. He was sitting in his study with two books lying open before him. One was on palmistry; the other was a medical book. He was examining his palm and comparing it to a diagram in the palmistry book. His vanishing life line was like a river that had dried up in the desert of his palm. In the medical book he looked at the pictures of darkening brains, the darkness increasing till nothing was left except the darkness. Beside the two books there lay on the desk a golden rectangle of light that the sun had cast through the room's only window. Half of the rectangle lay on top of the desk, half hung down along one side of it, as if its back had been broken by the edge of the upper surface.

He was thus preoccupied when his little son came running into the room.

'Dad,' he said, 'give me four *annas*, for the snake-charmer.' He got up to find some change, but by the time he had it the child was gone. So he went out to pay the man himself.

The snake-charmer was sitting in the verandah by himself. His young audience had dispersed and he was putting back the covers on the wicker baskets in which the snakes were carried. He was a young man, dressed in the customary saffron garb of his profession. His face was drawn like an ascetic's, with a straggling Mongol beard on his chin. He did not see the approaching man. So Mehdi said, 'Here!' extending his hand to give him the money. As he stood up, the eyes of the two men met and a shock went through Mehdi's frame as if someone had dashed a bucketful of icy water in his face. Transfixed, he gazed into the snake-charmer's eyes in birdlike fascination. The eyes were half open and completely motionless. There was an icy glitter in them. Inside those frozen pools Mehdi could see two pinpoints of light held still and unwavering, which made the eyes all the more unnerving. Yet one could not describe them as cruel eyes in the ordinary sense of the word 'cruel'. They were not the eyes of the feline species. Their pitilessness belonged to a higher order. They were angerless, aloof, and lordly.

Mehdi was thinking that the dark nature of his

profession had given them that unnatural look, when the man said, 'You are wondering about my eyes. In my travels with my snakes from city to city I come across people who remark upon how unusual they are. Some even ask me what I have done to them. Of course, I don't bother to satisfy their idle curiosity. But sometimes in the audience I notice troubled faces like yours, who deserve to be told—brothers in need of help, so to say. I catch them at the end of the show and tell them my story. So you see, I must tell my story to you too.' And he told him his story. In a way Mehdi was a willing listener, and yet in another, he knew he had no choice in the matter.

The snake-charmer's name was Abdul and his story went back a couple of years to the politically stormy days of 1947, when the British, after terminating their rule, were withdrawing from India, and the country was delirious with the fever of freedom. The energy of the nation, penned up in slavery for centuries and now suddenly released, went on a rampage. The joy of freedom lay in killing. Unable to vent their fury on their erstwhile masters, the two major religious communities, the Hindus and the Muslims, flew at each other's throats with a ferocity that staggered comprehension, and freedom was celebrated with the spilling of the blood of hundreds of thousands.

In this intoxicating game of murder Abdul found himself to be a masterful player. He planned and carried out his raids on the enemy territory with the efficiency of a military commander, systematically burning down one Hindu *mohalla* after another in the city. When the flames leapt high in scarlet joy against the night sky and the terror-stricken people fled in panic, he would be waiting for them with his men at the escape routes. The men were cut down, the children slaughtered, the young women were rounded up and raped in a mass orgy. Some of them had their breasts cut off and turned into fountains of blood.

With the cruelty of a tiger Abdul combined the cunning of a fox. The police were unable to catch him, and as to any other person capturing or killing him, the question did not arise. His eyes in those days were blood-shot and scorching red. They went into a man's soul and burned up his courage. How many times he had seen the hands of his enemies grow limp and drop their weapons even when they had caught him defenceless. He became known as Abdul-with-Death-in-his-Eyes. The title flattered him. At times he believed he was Death itself. Fear, of course, never touched him.

One evening, as the darkness deepened, his lieutenants assembled as usual at his house to take their orders. He spent some time with them discussing the night's target, and then went into an inner, dimly-lit room to fetch his gun that lay on a shoulder-high shelf. Still thinking of the strategy to be followed that evening, he grabbed at the gun. There was a furious hiss, which made him immediately let go and look up. There had been a cobra lying alongside the gun, which he had inadvertently caught. Now it had raised itself and was poised to strike, barely six inches away from his face. He tried to draw his head back, but the cobra leaned back too, ready to strike: the slightest movement on his part would trigger the spring. He froze. The cobra hissed and hissed furiously. The man without fear was now paralysed with a terror that he had never known before. At each whiplash of a hiss he trembled in his entire being. Eventually there was just an occasional hiss, and the two adversaries were motionless, face to face and peering into each other's eyes. The man felt that something was happening to his very eyeballs. He felt that the fiery vapour that had burned in them for months was fast cooling down. It dawned on him that this, and not the other battles, was the real encounter, in which he was proving to be a poor second. The real eyes of Death were in front of him now. He had only fooled himself when he believed that he was Abdul-with-Death-in-his-Eyes. He had been impertinent. He was only a poor human with life in his eyes.

He did not know how long he stood there. But as the red mist lifted from his eyes, he could see more clearly and with less fear. Before, he had seen a piercing point of light in each of the snake's eyes and shadows of anger crossing the eye-screens. Now he saw a whole world in them. A little sun hung in that universe and flakes of ashen snow dropped from its grey sky. He felt that he was wandering in that desolate landscape. He seemed to sense that countless others were there beside him, in the same plight. But he did not see them as, he felt sure, they did not see him. Everyone, he thought, felt that he was the only one existing in that lonely, silent world. He uttered a cry to break the immense silence, but the sound did not even travel to his ears—the air was dead. He touched himself, but there was no sensation. Desperately, he hit himself a hard blow; he did not feel where it landed. He looked into the stretching vastness before him, and something in him told him that if he penetrated the grey desert the scenery would change, and he would change too. There were distances, both inside and outside, to be explored. But as he started to move forward, the snake lowered itself and glided away.

He let a few minutes elapse; then he came out of the room, shading his eyes from his friends. Without looking at them he told them that he would not be able to accompany them that night. When they left, he left too, leaving the city for good. After that his only interest was in snakes. He travelled with them from place to place and told his story to those whom he considered worthy of hearing it.

The snake-charmer left and Mehdi returned to his study. He did not look at his books, nor even at the rectangle of light with the broken back, which anyway had almost disappeared. He did not turn on the light but sat in the growing darkness, his mind at ease. Something had happened that had taken away the agitation and the uncertainty of his mind. He sat there a long time, thinking of the snake-charmer's story, his eyes, and the world that was in them. When he went to bed he slept easily. As usual he woke up in the middle of the night, but this time there was no gnawing and whirring of the mind. The wall had not gone away. It was still there. But now he was confident that there were two little windows in it, probably as big as pinpoints, but that he should be able to find them. He fell back to sleep.

Next morning he got up, showered, had his breakfast, changed, and got ready to go out. He was acting like a man who knew what he had to do. He headed for the zoo. Once there, he sought out the reptile section and spent the whole morning standing before the glass cages of snakes.

The visit to the zoo became a daily, almost a religious routine for him. He would stand for hours looking at the snakes in the hope that one would lift its head and look into his eyes. Once in a while he was lucky to find a reared cobra behind the glass wall and he would fix his eyes on its eyes. But he did not see much, only a snake and its eyes. But he kept trying harder, concentrating. One day it happened that the snake disappeared and what he saw was a cottony blur in the middle of which was a black bud growing on a black stump.

The zoo-keeper was suspicious of him in the beginning, but seeing that he was a respectable-looking man, he tolerated him as an eccentric with a curious hobby. Then one day while he was sitting in his office he heard the tinkle of breaking glass. He came out. What he saw horrified him. There was that man by the king cobra's cage. He had broken the glass front and the reared cobra was barely six inches away from his face. The man did not move; the cobra did not move. They were frozen in a timeless balance. Then the keeper started running towards the man, his iron-tipped heels clattering on the cement floor. The man's head moved the slightest bit, turning towards the noise. The cobra struck. The man did not move, did not draw back. He stood like a pillar. The cobra struck again, like a velvet-covered hammer hitting his face. This time the man faltered and fell to the ground. The keeper reached him, dragged him away from the cage, and shouted for help. He cradled the wounded man's head in his lap. There were two deep bruises on his cheekbones under the eyes and beads of blood where the fangs had punctured the skin. What surprised the keeper was that the dying man's eyes were peaceful, even smiling.

AHMAD DIN GOES HUNTING

Ahmad Din had been on the train all night, sitting up, wedged between two passengers in the overcrowded railway compartment, and sleeping in snatches. The last time he had dozed off it was still night. But now when he opened his eyes the sun had risen. In the early morning light the surrounding country looked beautiful—wild, wooded and hilly. There should be plenty of game out there, he thought happily. That was what his friend Envar had told him—the place was swarming with wild life—and that was what had lured him to come to Ramgarh.

His left shoulder was aching. There was a man with an oversized head sitting next to him. Every time he woke up, Ahmad had found the heavy head of his neighbour resting on his shoulder, and every time he had angrily pushed it away, waking up its owner, who would dreamily apologize, even wanly smile, but would soon start leaning towards him the minute his eyes began to close. Now he thought with relief that he would not have to be a pillow for this inconsiderate man. In another half-hour he would be at his destination. Exactly at half-past six the train pulled up at Ramgarh Railway Station and he disembarked.

He had been sure that the first thing he would see on his arrival there would be the beaming face of his friend. Envar would be at the station to welcome him with open arms. But he wasn't there. Ahmad was disappointed. He strolled to the tea-stall for a cup of tea and then went into the Station Master's office to enquire about his friend's address.

In a small place everybody knows everybody else, and the Sub-Inspector of Police is a man of consequence. So when he asked the Station Master if he knew the Sub-Inspector, he said of course he did—one of his best friends and all that.

'Come for a shoot?' he asked, eyeing his gun.

'That's right.'

'Fine sport, shooting!' the old man remarked, and then, warming up, he added, 'Most exciting sport! Tiger once carried off a friend of mine, gun and all. Would you believe it?' Of course, he could believe it. But he thought it was hardly the proper thing to say. He hadn't come there looking for that kind of excitement. In fact he had tried to forestall such a situation: he had queried Envar to see if there were any dangerous animals there, and he had reassured him that there weren't any. So, as soon as he had extracted his friend's address from him, he left, and did not stay to listen to the gory details on which the old gabber was now fully launched—trail of blood, scattered limbs . . . . It took him ten minutes to walk to Envar's residence, and on the way he kept wondering if he had done the right thing in coming here. Envar had however assured him that Ramgarh was as safe as one's own backyard.

Not long since Envar had come, tracking an escaped felon, to Rajapur, where Ahmad Din lived and had stayed with him. The whole day he would be out playing Sherlock Holmes, but in the evening the two friends would sit down together and talk, especially of their college days. Those were happy times. There were four of them there, in the college residence—cronies, bosombuddies—eating together, reading together, and having fun together. Those were really great times, they agreed, and added with a somewhat forced conviction that even after college they hadn't done too badly in life. Envar was a Sub-Inspector of Police, Ahmad Din was an Assistant Station Master, the third was a mailman, and the fourth, who was the brightest of them all, had committed suicide, thereby solving all the lingering problems of life at one stroke. Their reminiscences made them nostalgic, and they often fell into long melancholic silences.

Coming out of one such silence, Envar said, apropos of nothing, 'You know, old man, you ought to get married.'

'How is that?' asked Ahmad.

'This is such a sleepy town, this Rajapur of yours, no fun, no interesting places! What do you do with yourself?'

'To tell you the truth, I don't have much of myself left after the night duty. And if ever I feel bored, I go out with my gun. That's what I do, although there isn't much to shoot around here.'

'Well, if you really like shooting you should come to Ramgarh,' Envar said.

'What will I do there? What is there to shoot?' he

said, dismissing Ramgarh summarily, although he knew nothing about the place.

'What is there to shoot?' his friend repeated in disbelief, 'I bet you haven't seen so many animals even in your dreams; the place is simply crawling with game.'

'Really?'

'Absolutely.'

'What? Hundreds of deer?' Ahmad's voice sang gaily, and a light came into his eyes, as in the forest of his imagination he saw countless antelope leaping about gracefully.

'Deer?' Envar rejoined, 'There are tigers and bears. . . .'

The rest Ahmad did not hear. The light faded from his eyes and the bounding bucks disappeared. 'Brother, you need a rifle for those things, and I've got only a twelve-gauge shotgun; besides, I don't think I can get leave. And above all,' he added, somewhat hesitatingly, 'the place seems to be dangerous.'

Envar laughed out loud, and said, 'I should have remembered; you were always such a coward.' Ahmad tried to say something by way of protest, but before he could do so, Envar added, 'Don't worry! The big game is in the far interior only, in the hills. My place is quite safe. I live at the edge of the forest, at the foot of the hills.'

Ahmad tried to explain his reluctance, but his friend wouldn't listen.

'You'll have to come,' he said, 'I won't take 'no' for an answer. And I guarantee that you'll return in one piece.'

Ahmad replied, 'All right, I'll come.'

And here he was, at Ramgarh, and Envar hadn't

even come to the station to receive him. Imagine his chagrin when he found, on reaching Envar's home, that he was away. An urgent call had come in the night and he had left in the early hours of the morning. He had told his servant that his friend would be arriving in a few hours and that he was to take good care of him.

'It was the *zamindar*'s daughter,' the servant volunteered.

'What about her? What did she do?' Ahmad asked idly.

'She ran off with a man last night.'

'Oh, did she?' he said, getting interested.

'Yes at midnight, when the whole household was fast asleep. The *zamindar* was all the more upset because she took the family jewellery with her, worth a hundred thousand rupees.'

'A hundred thousand! That's a lot of money.'

'Yes, that's what happened last night and Sahib had to go after them,' he said. 'And now Sahib, you must be hungry. I'll go and make you some breakfast.'

Latif, for that was the servant's name, wandered off to the kitchen, and Ahmad Din thought he would like to see the man who could cast such a spell on the gentler sex. As he thought about this a vague sadness descended upon him. He mused over the love of women and thought that not one woman had ever cast a loving glance at him. If she had, he would have been willing to lay down his life for her, even if she didn't bring any jewellery with her. But then women were such poor judges of men. They went by external looks; they never looked at the beauty of one's soul. As this train of thought tended to make him dejected, he decided to go out for a turn in the fresh air.

'Latif,' he called out, 'I'm going out for a few minutes, just to look around. I'll be back shortly.'

'All right, Sahib.'

'Any game around here?' he asked casually.

'Lots of deer, Sahib. Sometimes we can see them from the back of the house.'

This made him jump up, and he mechanically said, 'No!'

'Yes, Sahib, I'm telling the truth,' Latif replied.

Ahmad picked up his gun and went out, moving stealthily and keeping close to the side wall. Reaching the corner, he cautiously peered out to see if the deer were there that morning. But all he saw were a few hens scratching the ground, a sweeper-woman draining the cesspool, and a bearded goat pensively scanning the sky. He was disappointed. He looked up and saw a line of squat green hills in the near distance. Absent-mindedly, he started walking towards them.

In the space of half an hour he was there, among the hillocks. The vegetation was thick and thorny. As he walked up a little hill through the undergrowth, he tore his sleeve and pricked himself at three places in the course of fifty yards. But he went on, undaunted. He soon realized that there was no game to be seen anywhere. There were just a few monkeys hanging in the trees. Farther on he saw a few apes, and he said to himself, 'Brother, this is a monkey forest. The next thing you'll see will be a gorilla; so better beat it in good time.' And that was what he did. He turned round and began the downward climb.

As he came to the foot of the hill, he saw a villager in the distance. He hailed him, and when the man came up he asked, 'Where do you live?'

'There,' the man replied, pointing in the direction of some trees.

'What? In those trees?'

'No, behind them. There's a village behind them,' he explained.

'Oh,' Ahmad said and asked, 'Anything to shoot here?'

'Plenty of things.'

'What, for instance?'

'Sanbhar, deer, fox, jackal. . . .'

Ahmad listened with strained attention, waiting to catch the words 'tiger' and 'bear', but his informant stopped.

'Are there any bears or tigers?' he asked, to be doubly sure.

'No, Sahib, not in these parts. Once in a while one may come down from the far hills, but not as a rule. Oh, no! No tigers or bears!'

Ahmad felt relieved and told him that he had asked out of curiosity and had no other motive whatsoever. And to make the point more clear, he added, 'You know, I pity them, the poor tigers, being hunted by all those rajahs and maharajahs. If you kill them, you deprive the jungle of its walking beauty. I haven't the heart to destroy such beauty myself.' The man looked sceptical. These peasants, Ahmad thought, are nothing if they are not suspicious. So he changed the topic and said, 'Look here, if you beat a strip of the jungle and help me bag a sanbhar or deer, I'll give a rupee.'

'Four,' the man bartered. The bargain was clinched at two.

They examined the place strategically, and the

beater found him a spot to sit.

'You get into that bush, Sahib, and I'll start the beat from there,' he said, waving his hand towards a tall tree; some three hundred yards away. Ahmad stepped into the bush and the beater left. From his position he commanded the view of a clearing in the jungle. He sat there for some time, made sure that his gun was loaded, and then his eye fell on a thicker bush that was close by. Deciding it was a better screen, he got up and, leaving his cover, entered the other bush. Here he was perfectly hidden. An animal could saunter up to within a yard of him and not realize that it was already in the jaws of death. He was feeling excited and happy and impatient for the beat to begin.

In his excitement he felt a great desire to laugh, even to sing. But he controlled himself and waited in silence. He heard the beater call twice and then stop. He could not make out why. Then, as he changed his angle of vision by a few degrees, the reason became clear to him: it was standing there, at a distance of fifty yards from him, in the form of a fully-grown tiger.

A fuse blew in his mind and everything went black. He also felt that his heart had stopped beating, and then suddenly, for reasons known only to itself, it went into frantic action and beat everywhere in his body at the same time, including his fingernails, the tip of his nose, and each separate tooth.

The blackout lifted as fast as it had come and he saw the tiger start walking towards him, and he said to himself, 'Envar, brother, why did you call me here? Why did you want to kill me?' The tiger stopped. Ahmad was holding his breath and praying. The tiger advanced again and a pensiveness fell over the jungle; everything seemed to have gone into a swoon. The tiger stopped again, this time twenty paces from him, faced into the wind and sniffed.

'What is it smelling?' Ahmad asked himself. 'It can't be me. I had a shower only yesterday.' Then it occurred to him that it could be the jasmine oil in his hair. He promised to God that if he was spared this time, he would never put fragrant oil in his hair, in fact he would never use any hair-oil at all.

At this point it suddenly dawned on him that this bush was the tiger's lair and it was returning to it after a night's hunting in the hills. He thought he had been safe and secure in the other bush; why did he have to move into this one and lie in the tiger's bed? 'Come what may,' he said, ' let me fire the gun.' But it wouldn't go off; it was trembling even more than his hands. At this point, his consciousness began to flicker, and a voice within him said, 'Friend, it's a pity! You are taking a world of hopes and desires with you! Dying so young! Unmarried! Unloved! Unfulfilled!' And one scene of his life after another began passing before his mind's eye in a slow, mournful procession.

The tiger was now standing two yards from him and staring at him. Ahmad could not bear to look into those eyes, so he closed his own. Then the gun went off. A thunderous roar shook the forest, drowning the gun's report, and he fainted. But he could not even faint properly; he came to in a few minutes. He looked this way and that for the tiger, but it was not to be seen anywhere. He said to himself, 'Brother, run for your life while there is time. He's gone for a drink. He'll be back soon.'

So he picked up his gun, which had fallen to the ground, and started to leave the bush. A branch above him caught his collar. As he looked up to disentangle it, he saw the tiger. There it was, lying on top of the bush, right above him. He collapsed again and trembling set in afresh in every limb. However, two more minutes passed and he heard no movement. He looked up in slow motion; it was there all right. 'What's it doing up there?' he thought. 'Is it protecting me from the sun? Or does it want to humiliate me by urinating on my head?' No movement still! Very, very slowly he reloaded his gun and then emptied both barrels simultaneously into the belly of the tiger. This time there was no roar. He was now certain that it was dead. He came out of the bush.

After allowing himself some breathing time he called out to the beater. 'The swine!' he was muttering to himself, his anger mounting.

The beater came out of his hiding-place and, seeing the dead tiger, grinned from ear to ear, and said, 'What? You shot him?' The cup of Ahmad's forbearance overflowed and he flew at him, thumping him with the butt-end of the gun and saying, 'You swine, you almost murdered me! I asked you in the beginning. No bears, no tigers! Hunh? Your mother's this and that! Not even my body would have been found! Graveless! You...!' The wave of self-pity roused him to renewed effort.

When he had hammered him to his heart's content, he asked him to go to the village and bring help. When he returned, a crowd came with him. The tiger was slung on a pole and carried in a procession straight to the railway station for Ahmad had no desire to stay any longer at Ramgarh. At the station, surrounded by a flock of admirers, he waited for the train to come. He had placed one foot on the tiger, held the gun sloping in the crook of his arm, and was smoking with an air of unconcern as if what the public saw was not unusual for him. Inwardly, he was having a great time.

The train came and as chance would have it, the Burra Sahib, the boss of Ahmad's division, was on it. Noticing a crowd, he walked up to it to see if anything was wrong. He saw Ahmad standing at the centre of a circle of admirers. Recognizing him, for Ahmad had had part of his training under him only a year ago, he said, '*Babu*, who shot this tiger?'

'*Huzoor*, your humble servant did,' he replied. The Sahib was pleased and patted him on the back.

'Well done! How high was the *machan*?'

'*Huzoor*, we poor people can't afford *machans*. I shot him from the ground.'

'From the ground?' he repeated in amazement.

'Yes, *Huzoor*,' Ahmad admitted modestly.

'You must be very brave, then?'

'*Huzoor*, what can I say? It runs in the family.'

'Indeed! Indeed!' he said, and sat down to examine the tiger. 'You went for the forehead?' he said, with a trace of disapproval in his voice.

'*Huzoor*, I had to. I turned a corner and there he was, face to face with me. He saw me and bolted. I gave chase; he doubled back on me. The moment he pounced I fired. And there he was, rolling at my feet like a sack of potatoes. He died literally touching my feet,' he said.

The Sahib's eyes grew wide with wonder as he heard him describe the chase and the shooting of the tiger. 'How many have shot before?'

'*Huzoor*, it's not often that we poor people get a chance to go on a tiger hunt. This was my eleventh one.'

The Burra Sahib's sportsman's face beamed with pleasure. He shook Ahmad's hand, congratulated him and told him that he was very modest. Then he added, 'Next month I am going to Bengal on a tiger hunt. I'll take you with me.'

Ahmad shook from head to foot and said involuntarily, 'No, *Huzoor*!' His boss looked at him in surprise, so he quickly corrected himself, 'Too great an honour for me, *Huzoor*.'

'Not at all. I'd like you to come.'

'If that's your order, I'd be most glad to come. Thank you very much, Sahib.'

On the train all his newly found happiness deserted him. He was fearfully thinking that he was lucky to escape once. He couldn't escape twice. What was he to do? Then a bright idea struck him. He would write to the Sahib that he had had a change of heart and that now he believed that if you killed a tiger, you deprived the jungle. . . .

THE CLOWN

Professor Ramlal was a perfect example of the absent-minded professor. It was not unusual for him to discover that he did not have his reading glasses with him when he wanted to read out a passage to the class. He would look for them in all of his pockets. No, they weren't there; he'd left them at home. At times, instead of his glasses he would pull out the most unexpected thing from his pocket—for example, a sock. He would look at it in a most puzzled way. Then he would pull up his trouser legs to solve the mystery of the third sock, only to find that he was wearing only one. At this point the whole class, who had been watching his every move, would burst into laughter. He would shake his head and laugh too. Wildly amusing stories about him circulated in the college from time to time: thinking that the cigarette in his hand was a piece of chalk, he had tried to write with it on the blackboard, scattering a shower of sparks through the air instead of tracing letters on the board. Or, forgetting to pick up the pencil that he wanted to sharpen, he had painfully realized that it was his finger that he was sharpening. Not infrequently he would go into the wrong classroom. He was full of such aberrations, and when a colleague laughingly pointed out to him, for example, that his shirt cuff was hanging out a mile from his jacket sleeve, he would correct it and laugh himself. He always laughed on such occasions. Among his students and younger colleagues he was known as the clown.

This morning too, as he stepped into the classroom, his mind was wandering elsewhere. There was no one in the room, not a soul. For a moment he hesitated at the door: had he made a mistake again? Then he slowly recalled that the students had given a call for a strike for that day in connection with some grievance of theirs against the college. Every now and then they fought the authorities over one thing or another, often going on strikes, but a few had always shown up on such occasions. The classroom had never been empty, not in the last five years at least.

He went in, walked through the rows of empty seats to his dais, mounted it painfully, and sat down in his chair. He was a middle-aged man with stiff joints and dazzling white hair. His snow-white hair was, however, not a correct indication of his age: it made him look much older than he was. It is said that in order to look young one must try to feel young—defy time with desire—and that time is a fiery horse on which one must keep a tight rein. But Ramlal had long ago lost all interest in this business of keeping young. He had let the reins slip from his hands and the stirrups swing free from his feet, with the result that ,where one year had passed for the others, three or four had passed for him.

Now he was wondering why he had come into the

class at all, why he was sitting there and staring at the empty seats. It was a peaceful morning. Without the usual hustle and bustle of the students, the place was very quiet. He was on the fifth floor, and as he looked out through the tall open windows, he could see the green tree-tops and the upturned bowl of the sky. The sky was a deep blue and kites wheeled in the clear air. They looked like leisurely stains floating in the morning light. The minutes passed. Gradually, he felt a pain stir in his memory. It increased and made him dizzy. Darkness began to plunge before his mind's eye, and through it burst the stormy days of the 1942 uprising, when India had tried a violent overthrow of the British rule. Against this backdrop rose the picture of his son, Ramesh.

The boy had just finished a fiery speech in the Students' Union and was wiping his wet forehead, standing there on the rostrum. His face wore an expression that the father knew only too well. He was angry and determined to have his own way. Since his mother's death, when he was only seven, he would often be like that, hard to dissuade once he had set his mind on something. He would turn to stone before his father's remonstrances, and even remain unmoved by his pleas. Sometimes the father wondered where the child got his core of flint. Certainly not from him! Then he would smile and think of his wife. She had been a headstrong woman. All the same he had loved her, loved her deeply, and for the most part had yielded to her wishes. His own love was not self-assertive; he was content to be second in their relationship. And now he had loved his only child. Seeing that expression on the boy's face, his heart felt heavy with misgiving and he had a premonition of danger.

The days of the British rule in India were numbered, Ramesh had announced to his audience, and the time for the people to act had come. He had said that he could see the dark clouds of centuries roll away and the sun shining through. Let them join in a mighty effort to throw down the yoke of slavery. Let them turn this vast prison house into a land of the free. Their leaders had been arrested the previous day: Gandhi and Nehru and Azad were in jail, with hundreds of others. But they, the people, knew what their great leaders wanted from them; they expected them to do their duty. The fate of the future hung on the events of the next few days. Let them, he had exhorted his listeners, vow with their blood that they would not fail the country in its hour of need. From their blood would spring roses in a free India, and the eighth of August 1942 would go down as one of the greatest days in the history of the motherland.

The speech concluded and the air exploded with cries of death to the rulers and victory to Mother India. The speaker's words had turned the student body into a raging animal that swayed uneasily but did not know what to do with itself.

Another boy mounted the rostrum. He spoke calmly, in an unanimated voice. After Ramesh he seemed to be a speaker from another planet. He did not speak of the sun and the roses. Instead, in measured tones and businesslike phrases, he suggested a simple line of action. There was no one to guide them, he began, as their leaders were in prison. But before their arrest they had made it clear that the British must quit India, and that from now on it was a war to the knife. Those were Mahatma Gandhi's very words. Under the circumstances at home and with war going on in Europe and Burma, the only way to force the hand of the rulers was to paralyze the administration here in India. News was coming in fast and furiously that the people had taken that course. Railway tracks were being torn up, telephone wires cut, and government buildings set on fire. They could do no better than to follow that example. Let them go and set fire to the city law courts.

Although the fever and excitement of the crowd had considerably abated during this matter-of-fact speech, yet a roar of assent greeted the suggestion. It was decided that the students should march in a body to the District Law Court Building and burn it down to the ground. The college clock was striking the hour of eleven when the crowd of young men and women set out to do or die.

In half an hour they were there. A number of armed policemen were guarding the place. The authorities, anticipating trouble, had taken strong protective measures. As the mob of students drew near, the armed guard fell into line, and their commander, stepping out, shouted to them not to proceed any further. Stubbornly, the crowd of young people pressed on, more in defiance than in accordance with any strategy. Once again the officer warned them and threatened to shoot if they did not stop.

This time the crowd came to a halt, six feet from a low hedge that marked the boundary of the Courts. For a brief period a buzz went round the mass of students; then some clear voices rose. Some suggested that the marchers should turn around and return to strike at a more opportune moment: why allow the government butchers to slaughter them? Others said that they were not cowards; British bullets had never stopped them before, so why should they stop now? Still others shouted to the armed men that they too were Indian; would they shoot at their own brothers and sisters?

Then Ramesh detached himself from the crowd. There was black determination in his face. As his father, who had followed the procession, saw him, his heart stood still. He wanted to shout 'No!' to him; in fact, the cry rang in his mind, but no sound came out. The young man turned to the crowd and said that the question of turning back did not arise. Were they to be found wanting in the very first moment of trial? He said that they should not advance in a body, but one by one. Let the mercenary dogs slaughter them. By evening a thousand corpses would surround them, a thousand martyrs at the altar of the country's freedom—their blood would not have been shed in vain. He himself would give the lead; the rest would follow.

He advanced toward the hedge. The commander shouted, 'Don't cross, or I'll shoot.' His men shouldered their rifles, and the young man went over the hedge. A shot rang out. The young man clutched at his breast and fell convulsively to the ground. The shock of what had happened dumbfounded the crowd for a few seconds. Then the tight thread of silence snapped. A groan lifted from the crowd and disintegrated it. Men ran here and there, cursing, shouting; women shrieked, some sobbed, some collapsed. Three men rushed to help their fallen comrade. The policemen stood with grim faces, still at the ready. The crowd dispersed.

The wounded man was quickly thrown into a tonga and rushed to the college hospital. The father was paralyzed with fear, perceiving things as if they were happening at a great distance from him, in a dream. In the hospital he waited outside the operating room, in a trance, far beyond the reach of his own senses. The doctor came out and asked him to go in. He went in, and the doctor turned to the anxiously waiting crowd and said, 'He has no chance; he's dying.'

The boy was fighting for breath. His eyes were open—large and dark with pain. His face and hair were wet with perspiration. The father took his hand in his and held it tightly. 'Father, I don't want to die,' he said, his voice weak and pleading. The father's grip tightened. He sat like a statue, mute, with tears trickling down his face, as he watched his son through a quivering film. What could he do? If he were a god, he would have crushed India in the palm of his hand to give him back his life. As it was, he was helpless, and in his helplessness the tears flowed from his eyes and fell on the tightly clasped hands. A convulsion shook the boy's frame and his hand grew limp.

For days after that, Ramlal went about in a stupor. When people talked to him, their words did not reach him; and later, when they did, and he heard them talk of heroism and martyrdom, he wanted to be angry with them and tell them that no country was worth a man's blood. His friends were very kind to him. They would console him in his grief, and then they would talk in glowing terms of his son and his supreme sacrifice. As they did this, their voices changed, grew rich with the warmth of tribute, and took on the tone of celebration.

He could not doubt the sincerity of their feelings. It was transparently clear that they felt great respect, pride, and admiration for his son, but he himself felt nothing of the kind, only stark grief and desolation, and sometimes anger. Gradually, the pressure of their praise made him confused. Were his feelings fighting his son, or what remained of him—a glorious memory? He lay awake at nights, relived the tragedy of that day again and again, saw the faces of his friends, heard their words in his mind, and he wrestled in the inner night of his self with the question: was he opposing his son's sacred memory with his personal grief? The others had bowed to his destiny with grace, why shouldn't he? It seemed to him that his selfish grief was like a floating stain in a clear morning. And he made the decision against himself. He would try to overcome his grief and offer Ramesh something better than the emptiness of his heart. Once again he had placed himself second in love.

His unexpected return to work surprised his colleagues. There were no classes in the remaining days of August; the students were too busy with politics to come to college. But the orders from the government to the faculty were that they were to go to their classes, students or no students. If they did not, they would be fired, or worse. The principal would certainly have made an exception in Ramlal's case and explained it to the higher authorities, but there he was, day after day, sitting through the empty hours and staring at the invisible class. People said how brave he was—a brave father of a brave son. He hid his feelings.

It had been five years now since he first had tried to forget his grief, but he had not been successful. Instead, he had forgotten himself. Speaking practically, it amounted to the same thing: if the image won't go away, fog the mirror; the result is the same. And speaking socially, there was another result: he had become a hypocrite. But as his

72

motives were self-effacing, he had become the only lovable hypocrite in nature—a clown—without even knowing it.

The bell rang and awoke him from his reverie. He rose slowly and left the room. As he entered the faculty common room, carrying a load of books and an attendance register under his arm, all eyes were turned toward him.

'You were in class?' a young colleague asked.

'Yes.'

'Lecturing to empty benches?' he enquired smilingly.

'No, I forgot. . . .'

'You forgot that nobody was there?' he cut in and laughed.

Ramlal did not complete his sentence, as everyone was now laughing. He laughed with them.

GRANDMA

Aziz Manzil, old and grey, standing by the railway tunnel, was our house. I say 'was' because it is no longer ours. After the partition of India, most of my people left the country and went to Pakistan. Those who had stayed behind followed them in two years' time, and our property was alienated by the government of India.

The passage to our house lay through a narrow, paved lane. The lane, which served as a playground for the children of the neighbourhood, was flanked by two high walls that cut off the sun's rays and kept the lane in constant shade and half-light. Twenty yards down the alley-way was an old archway; this was the entrance to our house. Along one side of the lane ran an open drain that carried black, smelly water. Once a week the municipal sweeper came on his sanitary mission, and all the children gathered round and watched him run forwards and backwards with his broom dipped in the water. This was his idea of a cleaning job. It only made the drain look dirtier than before. The dark mud that lay at the bottom would be churned up and the foul smell that always hung in the air would be intensified.

But we did not mind these things. The smell did not bother us and the muddy water was all right as far as we were concerned. A hundred times a day our ball would roll into the drain, and we retrieved it with our fingers without the least hesitation. If a grownup person happened to be going by at that time, we waited for him to pass, or fished out the ball with our bare toes. We did not expect anyone to find fault with that.

The lamp-lighter came at sundown to light the single lamp in the lane, carrying a slender ladder on his shoulder and a lantern in his hand. We children never stopped to watch him at his work as we did the sweeper, because he came at dusk; and the lane, quite dark by that time, held unknown terrors for us. At the far end of the lane was an empty house with broken walls and caved-in roofs. Heaps of broken bricks lay in its courtyard; and in the middle of the rubble stood a magnificent plum tree, which looked fantastic in that setting in the daytime, but sinister at night.

It was generally believed that spirits and djinns haunted ruins, and the wrecked house in our lane was no exception. Every fifteen days or so, and always on a Thursday night, some thoughtful member of our community would light a little lamp—a tiny saucer of oil with a floating wick in it—in honour of the spiritual creatures, and to keep them in good humour. Also an *anna*'s worth of sweetmeats was placed by the lamp. This was dinner for the spirits. They fed on its smell.

Sometimes, on Friday morning, we would see bits of sweetmeat in a niche of the ruin; and in the tiny saucer would be a black stain left by the burnt-out wick. We used to fight among ourselves for every plum that dropped from the tree, but none of us had the courage to touch the left-overs of the djinns. They might get offended and then sure disaster would follow. There was at least one victim of their wrath, or so we believed. He was a boy of fourteen, much older than the boys of our age group. His name was Irshad. It was said that as a child he would sometimes steal the sweetmeats offered up to the djinns. This angered them. So one summer's night, when it was warm and he was sleeping on the roof, they lifted him from his bed and flung him down. He was picked up unconscious, and with a broken leg. His leg was now all crumpled, and he went on crutches.

So, at dusk I would return home. Nasiban would be hunting for the lanterns. It was time to light the lanterns, and she could not find them. 'Arif, son, please find the lanterns for me. I don't know why they can't be left at their places,' she would say when she saw me. It was the easiest thing for me to find them. I would bring them to her one by one. She sat on a little platform in the courtyard with a bottle of kerosene oil, a few rags of cloth and a handful of ashes by her side. After I had brought all the lanterns I would sit down and watch her slowly detach the chimneys and polish them with rag and ash. I was absolutely forbidden to touch the chimneys for fear I should break them. Then the lanterns were filled up, and if the kerosene ran out, it was my special pleasure to go and work the suction pump and fill the bottle from the large oil can.

Nasiban was our woman servant. She did the household chores and went on errands to the market. She looked terribly old and wrinkled to me, and her dark brown skin was as tough as leather. I remember once the cholera broke out in the city, and the government inoculator came to inoculate us. When it was Nasiban's turn, the needle would not go into her skin, and the man said he would have to go and get an awl to make a hole. Although she was old, Nasiban was an indefatigable woman, and was on her feet from morning to evening.

As she polished the chimneys, she talked to me, mostly about her family. She had a married daughter at Rampur and a son working in Delhi. I listened, but with half an ear. I was more interested in watching her take the lanterns to pieces and put them together again; and the special moment when she put the light to the wick and a soft, golden flame sprang up in the crystal-clear chimney. When the lanterns had been lit, I would dispose them about the house, swinging them back to their right places.

One lantern I took to Grandma. If she was on the point of finishing her evening prayers, she would motion to me to come to her. She would hold my face between her flabby hands, repeat a few Arabic words, and breathe a blessing on me. Then she would be free to talk: 'Where have you been the whole day? You did not come to me even once.'

'I was busy, Grandma.'

'Oh, you were busy! I suppose you go to work like your uncle?'

I forgot to mention that I was eight years old at that time. 'No, Grandma, but I have a lot of other things to do.'

'I know your things. You play the whole day in the lane.' Then she would ask me to get her a jar from her cupboard, from which she gave me cookies.

I had seen Grandma for the first time a year before. My father, a law officer in Bhopal, had been killed in an accident, and my mother had come to Agra to live with her people. Now, Grandma was not my grandmother. She was my mother's grandmother. But as everybody called her Grandma, I did as well. She was all white: her hair, eyebrows, skin, and clothes were of the same colour. She was terribly old. Her skin hung in loose folds from the bone. She scared me at first. When, on our arrival from Bhopal, she asked me to come to her, I refused and clung to my mother. And when my mother tried to force me to go to her, I began to cry. 'Let him be,' said Grandma, and my mother let me alone, feeling too weak to assert her authority after her recent bereavement.

But Grandma knew how to deal with me. She plied me with sweetmeats, and in a few days my conquest was complete. Soon I was sitting near her, playing, while she said her prayers. And when she had finished, she would always give me sweets. Sometimes, my uncle remonstrated with her, saying that stale sweets were not good for me. She would become sulky and grumble to herself: 'How can sweets be bad for children?' And I would be inclined to agree with her.

One day Grandma complained of some trouble in her ear. She felt as if an insect had got in it. She could hear it move, she said. She asked Nasiban to call a *singiwalla*—a professional ear-cleaner. I had never seen an ear-cleaner before. He had a turban coiled on his head, and sticking in its folds were half a dozen metal pins and a dozen swabs. In his hand was a bottle-holder with four little bottles of fragrant oils fitted into it. Round his neck was a string from which hung a hollow horn—the horn giving the man the name of *singiwalla*. Grandma told him of her complaint. The man probed the ear with a pin, put his eye to the ear, and shook his head.

'What is it?' asked Nasiban, 'is it wax?'

'No,' said the man. 'It's not wax, it's earwigs.' He peered into her ear again and said he could see them. I also took a peep, but I could see nothing. He put the cylindrical horn to Grandma's ear, and sucked. She flinched as the vacuum hurt her ear. Then he tapped out two earwigs on the floor from the horn. And then one more came out. After that he put two drops of oil in Grandma's ear, and charged four *annas*. Grandma felt much better.

The whole day I went about in fear of earwigs, and in the evening when my uncle returned and told me that Grandma's ailment was imaginary and that the ear-cleaner was a fraud, and that earwigs do not live in the ear, I did not believe him. He said that in old age the eardrum gets a little dry, and sometimes the movement of the head shakes it and one gets that crawling sensation. All the same, when I went to bed that night, I lifted my pillow to see if earwigs were hiding there to get into my ear. Every six months Grandma called the ear-cleaner, and he never failed to produce the earwigs.

Grandma was her own physician, and the most amusing of her cures was for constipation. About a month after my arrival, I was amazed one day to see her with an unlit cigarette in her hand. She called me to come and sit next to her. She was going to smoke. It was incredible. I had never seen a woman smoke before. So I looked up in doubt at my mother and uncle, but they did not seem to mind. Later on, Grandma told me the medicinal purpose behind the smoking. The idea was that if one swallowed the smoke, it would exert a pressure on the bowels and push out whatever was clogging them. So the smoke had to be swallowed and kept inside, and it was here that my help was needed. She would hold her nose and I was to keep her lips pressed together with my fingers, so as not to allow the smoke to escape. She then would light the cigarette and take a pull, but before either of us could do the holding the smoke was gone. It blew out. The next time we were quick, she clinging to the nose, I to the lips. Then it was I to the nose and she to the lips; but the greater part of the smoke always dribbled out in little threads and coils from the corners of her mouth. I enjoyed myself immensely at this game, and she would say good-naturedly: 'What is there to laugh at, you little monkey?'

Sometimes an ailment would defy her diagnosis and not respond to her treatment. Then I would be sent to the apothecary's, repeating the symptoms to myself on the way. The apothecary was a very fat man, and I always felt he was another squat, big, clay jar among the innumerable jars that filled his shop.

'Raj Singh, Grandma needs medicine,' I would say.

'What's the matter with her?' he would ask.

I would recount what little I remembered, and would come back with some herb or dried plums twisted up in a bit of paper with 'to be boiled and taken at bedtime' pencilled on it. Sometimes it would be a syrup to be taken with iced water; it strengthened the heart. Even during a serious illness Grandma never consented to see a doctor. She had a deep-rooted suspicion of everything Western.

Grandma's chief occupation was to pray, which she did day and night. In the winter, when I went to bed early and struggled to lie awake to hear the nine o'clock train go through the tunnel, I would poke my head out of the blanket and look at Grandma. She would be sitting motionless like a picture on the prayer-carpet. And in the morning, if I happened to wake before sunrise, I could hear her monotonous drone, as she read the Quran. The whole house would be asleep and plunged in darkness, but in her corner glimmered a lantern as she sat before the holy book.

I asked my mother why Grandma prayed so much. She said, 'Hers has been a sad life, and when one is sad one wants to pray.'

I always cried when I was hurt or unhappy, so I said, 'Why doesn't she cry?'

'She has cried a great deal,' said my mother reflectively. 'Even now when her sorrow revives, she cries.'

I was unable to understand my mother's words fully until a few months later. The summer had come, and we slept in the courtyard, under the sky. One warm and oppressive night I got up for a drink of water. As I lay down again, I watched my mother and wondered how she could work the hand fan when obviously she was asleep. All of a sudden I heard a low moan as if someone were in great pain. I drew close to my mother for protection, and heard. It was Grandma crying in her sleep. As she cried she started to sing. The song penetrated me with a deep sense of fear and uneasiness. I could not follow the words, as they were broken with sobs, but I noticed that Grandma's voice had become much younger. It seemed the voice of a girl.

In my panic I woke my mother. She listened for a moment and hushed me to silence. 'She's dreaming, poor thing!' she said.

My fear having vanished with my mother's waking,

I felt the wailing song fill my heart with sadness, and I started crying. Presently the song subsided, but the dry sobs continued after brief silences, and finally they ceased.

In the morning when I got up my head was full of the night's experience. I asked my mother why Grandma cried like that. She said, 'She dreamed of her married life and her husband. He left her after a year of their marriage.' She stopped for a bit and then said, 'Do you know how old Grandma is?'

'No,' I said.

'She is over ninety. She was married at sixteen, a year later my mother was born, and Grandma's husband went off with a low woman and never came back.'

Grandma was married at sixteen. There were only two men in the home to which she had come: Grandma's husband and his father, Syed Aziz Ali, after whom Aziz Manzil was named. Aziz Manzil was not then what it is now. It was a two-room house with a courtyard in front. As the prosperity of the house grew, so did Aziz Manzil, till it became an unplanned, sprawling monster, containing within its being all the phases of it evolution. In the oldest wall, in the courtyard, were two big iron nails, driven into the wall by Aziz Ali's own hands. They were among the family heirlooms, and every year, before the rains set in, they received a fresh coat of paint to prevent them from rusting.

Grandpa, so the legend went, was a very handsome man in his youth. My mother told me stories she had heard about him. He was handsome as a prince, and had an athletic build. He could run as far as Sikandra and back, which came to ten miles. He assisted his father, who was a copyist in the law court, at his work. Grandma kept house and cooked. When father and son came back in the evening, and had washed, she would serve them their dinner. As they ate, she sat with them, fanning them. When dinner was done, Aziz Ali sat in front of his house, smoking a *hookah* and talking about the day's events with friends who happened to drop in. Grandpa went out to visit friends or just for a stroll in the market-place. He returned by ten. Grandma, having eaten and finished the washing up by then, would be waiting for him. Then they would lie down and talk. I wish I knew what they said, but it must have been something pleasant, for both were young, handsome, and healthy. A girl was born to them after a year of their marriage.

One night Grandpa returned home very late. He had gone to attend a marriage in the neighbourhood, where after the feast the guests were entertained to a *nautch*. Sitara, the then celebrated dancing-girl had come. She was a little brown woman with the easy movements of a tigress and big, bold eyes, whose power she knew. Rajahs and nawabs invited her, and she charged the fantastic sum of five hundred rupees for a performance. The music started, and with a stamp of her foot, which set all the little silver bells tied to her ankle tinkling, she released something powerful and intoxicating into the atmosphere—the dance was under way. Grandpa watched her, spell-bound, with a stupid, half-forgotten smile on his face and fire coursing in his veins. The girl too was struck with his appearance, as he sat there like a prince in that crowd. With overly bold movements of her body she came towards him and receded like a tantalizing wave. It was in a dazed condition that Grandpa came home that morning at three o'clock. Grandma and the child were sleeping peacefully.

The next day he went off with the dancer, never to return. Aziz Ali was furious. He raged and fumed and swore that he would shoot him if he ever set foot in his house. And the poor man wept in secret over the disgrace that his son had brought to the fair name of the family by going off with a low woman. However, he continued to go to work, smoked his *hookah* in the evening, but stopped seeing people. Towards Grandma he grew infinitely tender and considerate. Seeing her go about like a dumb, wounded animal, he would sometimes place his hand over her head and say: 'He is dead. It's good it is so. Forget him, daughter. God has given you a child; look after her. As long as I am alive. . . .' but seeing Grandma's fast-flowing tears, he would stop short and go away.

Grandma had not been prepared for this suffering. She had been dropped in mid-air, so she found her grief insupportable. Every night she cried herself to sleep, and her strong, healthy body became a torture to her. It was in this condition that she turned to God, and from the age of seventeen to over ninety, till her death, did nothing but pray. She did not know what was going on in the world outside. She did not even know that a world existed outside the confines of our *mohallah*. Wars shook the world, India passed through a tumultuous period of her history, and Grandma did not even know who Gandhi was. The only politics she knew was that the crafty *Firangis* had stolen the throne of Delhi from a Muslim ruler, when she herself was a little child, and that there were still Muslim rulers in Bhopal and Hydrabad, where most of her grandsons served.

Seventy-five years of prayer—girlhood, womanhood, middle age, old age, all nailed to the cross! It makes me shudder now to see in my mind those vast seventy-five years stretching endlessly, and Grandma sitting motionless on the prayer-carpet, with a dim lantern burning near her, and she turning from a beautiful, rosy-cheeked girl into a wrinkled hag of over ninety. I do not believe in God myself, but sometimes I do think that there must be some small corner in this infinite universe where all the prayers can go.

Grandma believed like a child in Heaven and Hell and the Day of Judgement. 'I shall demand justice from the Lord on the Day of Judgement,' sometimes she would say. No, Grandma, do not demand justice from your Lord, otherwise your beloved husband for whom you cried in your sleep for seventy-five years, will be consigned to the everlasting flames. That will not make you happy. Make your Lord give him a beating, a most sound beating, and when he has been hurt enough and he has cried enough, ask Him to make you seventeen years old and him twenty, the age when you lost him. And although there will be no Aziz Manzil in Heaven, still find a quiet corner, and when it is night and the stars are shinning, talk to each other, picking up the thread where you left off at seventeen.

Javed Ali felt in his sleep that he was being watched.
Two ghostly eyes were fixed on him and were penetrating
the barrier of closed eyes that protects a sleeping man
from the outside world. He could see them like the
headlamps of a car in a fog. The experience gave him an
eerie feeling and he woke up with a start, only to find that
he wasn't dreaming. The eyes were still there, searching
his face. They were his wife's.

He was annoyed. He could see Sophie only vaguely,
for the early morning light was still dim in the bedroom.
She had drawn herself up and was sitting propped up
against the head of the large bed, a little away from him.
Her face was turned in his direction and her big eyes were
fastened on him in a steady gaze.

'What is it?' he asked vexedly. 'You gave me a
start.'

She had given him an unpleasant turn and he made
no attempt to hide his annoyance; his voice was rude. He
turned over, shut his eyes and loosened his body in a fresh
surrender to sleep, when he heard her voice come weakly

over his shoulder, 'I'm sorry, darling. I didn't mean to disturb you.' He mumbled something. She spoke again, slowly, 'I had a dream.' He felt her voice sounded different—strained, breaking.

'Oh, did you?' he responded sleepily.

'I haven't slept since then,' she said.

'Overate last night?' he asked facetiously.

'It was about you,' she replied in a serious tone, ignoring his attempt at humour.

'About me? What about me?' he said, turning over and opening his eyes.

'I saw you lying with Ram Kali.'

For a moment he lay quiet, unable to grasp her meaning; then, realizing the full implication of her words, he cried, 'What?'

'I am sorry, darling,' she said, 'I've been feeling very badly myself; I cried.' Javed looked at her thoughtful, tear-stained face.

'I never heard such nonsense.'

'I got up frightened. I've been looking at you and I felt I couldn't touch you,' she said.

'I never heard such rot. You go and dream a silly dream, you insult me, and then you hate me and don't want to touch me.'

'Yes, it's all very foolish,' she replied in a faltering voice and again began to cry.

'Now what's all this Sophie? Don't be silly! How can you even think of such a thing?' he asked, wiping her tears and holding her face in his hands.

She smiled. 'I am very silly.'

'That you are,' he said, and kissed her.

Ram Kali was a low-caste sweeper-woman, who

came to sweep out the rooms and clean the outdoor lavatory. Jet black in colour, she was about thirty years of age. She tied a broad band of cloth tightly over her sari around her waist, which accentuated the vulgar swing of her big hips when she walked. The hips protruded backwards as much as her big breasts stuck out forwards. Her face was big and coarse, and her rough skin stretched tightly over her fat, bursting cheeks. There were gaps between her square, yellow, strong teeth, and her thick cracked lips were always stained a rust colour from her constant chewing of *pan*. She came every morning and evening, did her work quietly and left. Mostly the Alis did not even notice when she came and went.

This was Ram Kali, and being sexually coupled with her in his wife's imagination came as a great shock to Javed. In the course of the day, while he was at work, his mind repeatedly went back to the morning scene. It seemed especially ironic to him that the one thing that should not have been doubted—his absolute devotion to his wife—had been questioned. How could she suspect him of infidelity even in a dream? In the eleven months that they had now been married, didn't she see in his eyes, hear in his voice, what she meant to him? He recalled the anxious days when he was pressing for the hand of this beautiful seventeen-year-old with her parents, and how they had taken a long time in replying. But they had finally accepted his proposal. After his marriage he had told his wife that she was his dream come true. And he had sincerely meant every word of it. She was everything that his senses could have desired. She was a fragrance in his nostrils, a vision in his eyes, and a heaven in his arms. In the darkness of the bedroom her silvery form gleamed like that of the moon-goddess in the night-sky. The sea of his passion rose and fell and dashed itself on the rocks in violent ecstasy, till its power was spent and it lay heaving at the feet of the goddess, bathed in her soft light.

Only when he was falling asleep after the love-making would he feel a little irked that Sophie had not responded to his ardour. She had submitted rather than participated. But that was all right, he thought. She was still very young. And he was also aware of the fact that he was not her dream man. She did not have the same feelings towards him as he had for her. But he was confident that, seeing his frank adoration of her beauty, she would in due course grow fond of him and joyously wrestle with him on such occasions. He just had to be patient. Besides, there was no reason for hurry, no cause for complaint at present, for when he held his wife in his arms his happiness was so complete that he was not aware of anything else, not even of the feelings, or the lack of them, of his love-partner.

It is true that Sophie did not reciprocate her husband's feelings for her. Hers had been an arranged marriage, at least in the spirit if not in the strict traditional form. She had been able to see Javed three or four times before they were married. Dinner parties had been arranged at mutual friends' houses, where the two of them were thrown together. They had exchanged a few words too. She didn't like him as the man she would like to marry. Her parents were disappointed.

They were very keen on the match. They admitted that he was not the handsomest of men, that he was twelve years older than Sophie. But he had a number of strong points. He came of a good family, was of sound character, was well-to-do, and above all, was very well placed. He would take very good care of his wife. Their daughter would be in good hands. So when she showed her unwillingness, they did not hide their disappointment. Of course, they would not force her, they said, to marry anyone against her wishes. The final decision in this matter should be hers. However, they would ask her to give the matter a little more thought and not reject the offer out of hand. Should she change her mind they would be delighted. With their youngest daughter well-settled, they would have discharged their last major responsibility. A great load would be lifted from their minds, and they could look forward to a peaceful old age. Sophie promised to reconsider the matter.

She talked to her aunt Alia about her dilemma. Being her favourite niece, she was close to and open with her. In turn Alia was concerned and sympathetic towards Little Sophie, a childhood name that she affectionately continued to use even when her niece was no longer little but a strapping young woman. She was especially sensitive to Sophie's present situation for she too had been pushed into a loveless marriage. By social standards she had done well. She was the wife of a high-ranking Government officer, was widely respected in the city, and was welcomed wherever she went. Even on a personal level she had, to a large extent, fulfilled herself. She had two adorable children, had worked towards and won a university degree after her marriage. But she failed to love her husband. The fertile field of man-and-woman relationships in which so much could have grown had lain fallow. She had found no joy as a wife. At thirty-five, fifteen years after her marriage, she was still stunningly beautiful, and her husband even now came to her like a thirsty animal to a stream of cold water. But her own heart was not involved in what he did. He would go up in flames but rarely succeed in lighting a fire under her. A few years after their marriage he told her that she was aloof and cold like the moon. She heard the rebuke in silence, thus in a way accepting the blame. But neither she nor her husband saw the injustice of the remark: it is not the moon on which the sea directs its fury, only on its image. Whereas Alia lay rumpled and crumpled in bed.

Alia talked to her brother against the intended match. He listened but was not convinced.

'You are a romantic Alia. Does love at first sight ensure a happy marriage?' he asked.

'No, it doesn't,' she agreed, 'but a disinclination at first sight makes a happy marriage almost impossible.'

'Happiness in marriage,' he continued, 'is not found. You have to work for it. What is needed is understanding and tolerance. Physical attraction is a passing thing. It may bring two people together, but it's not going to hold them together,' and so on.

Alia was unable to convert her brother to her point of view. It seemed all the more strange to her that he should talk like this when he and his wife had married for love. They were cousins and had loved each other since they were children. She was herself a child when they had married, but she still remembered their ecstatic faces. As in the life of any married couple, there were, later on, differences of opinion between them, quarrels, even periods of severely strained relations. But the initial warmth and affection that had existed between them had always returned, like underground water seeping up to moisten the dry land.

'Doesn't my brother see a continuity in his married life?' she asked herself. 'Doesn't he see the root from which the flowers and the fruit have grown? Why has the golden summer of youth totally receded from his memory and turned unreal and imaginary in the season when it is time to bring in the harvest? Is the harvest time the only season of life? I guess I'd be the same when it is time for my Little Yasmin to get married. No, I won't. My brother has known love and forgotten it. I have not known love, but I will never forget it. I'd never be like him.'

Finally, Sophie gave in to the wordless pressure. Nothing was said, but she knew how keenly her parents were awaiting the right reply. She told them she would marry Javed.

A few months after the wedding, niece and aunt talked again, this time of conjugal intimacies. Alia smiled ruefully; she didn't have to be told. In the end she said, 'No, Little Sophie, you can't do anything except to submit and let him work his will.' She also went on to explain that a man's love was not the whole of a woman's life. In due course, the children would come; they would fill a large part of her life. Also, she should go back to school to complete her education. Then there was the Women's Association, of which Alia was the President. She could join it. They did a lot of social work in the community, especially with the women and the children, and the meetings of the Association were really interesting. Sophie joined the Women's Association.

A month had passed since Sophie's dream and Javed had almost forgotten it, and had returned to his former abandon in loving his wife. Then one day he woke to find his wife upset and in tears. It was the same dream again, she said.

'What is this?' said Javed, feeling deeply hurt. 'Don't you realize how bad it makes me feel? I'll start hating myself. You make me feel guilty for nothing. Sophie, don't you see how debasing it is to me?'

'I'm sorry, darling,' she said, 'I never meant to tell you. You shouldn't have woken up.'

'I know I shouldn't have, but I did, and I feel rotten, angry. Look, we'll fire that Ram Kali.'

'No, no,' she said, 'how is she to blame?'

'But then you won't have that dream when she's gone,' he said.

'No, no, it'll stop by itself. Besides,' she added with a laugh, 'what reason will you give her? Will you tell her of my dream?'

Javed felt hot all over at the idea, and said nastily, 'I don't have to give reasons to a servant. I'll just turn her out.'

'All right, all right, you'll turn her out,' she said, regaining her cheerfulness. 'Now who's getting upset? You tell me I get upset for nothing and now you are getting upset yourself.'

He didn't say anything to this, but he could not regain his composure. She asked him if he remembered that today was their wedding anniversary. Of course he did, he said. They had asked a few friends and family members over to tea in the afternoon. Javed had to pick up the cake that Sophie had ordered from the bakery , and also cigarettes and *pan* for the guests.

'Don't be late,' she said, when he was leaving for the office.

'No,' he said.

His mood did not improve the whole day. The disgust and the anger kept simmering in him. If one could have seen with the eye of one's imagination, one would have seen a scowling devil in a black cloud hovering over Javed's head. His subordinates in the office did not see the devil over him, but they knew that the Sahib would pounce on them at the least little mistake; so they kept out of his way.

The party went off very well. There were plenty of people, plenty of flowers, plenty to eat and drink, and much laughter. Sophie looked more attractive than ever. She had a red sari on, and her face was animated and eyes shining. Javed loved her and hated her too. His devil had retreated but not retired.

It was getting dusk when the party broke up. There was a great deal of hand-shaking, humorous remarks, and good wishes, till everybody left except Alia. She and Sophie sat talking together, and Javed busied himself with the newspaper. Then the two women got up and said they were going to the Women's Association meeting. Sophie said to Javed that she would be a little late as she would be dining with Aunt Alia and that he should not wait up for her. Then they left.

Javed got up and walked aimlessly to the door. Through the doorway he saw Ram Kali sweeping the verandah. It gave him a bit of a shock to see her. He stood watching her. Her bare forearm, strong and round like a rolling-pin, shook at every stroke of the straw-broom, as she moved briskly, bent over her work. Her left cheek was stuffed with *pan*, which she chewed like an animal chewing the cud. Her dirty maroon blouse was stretched tight over her firm, fleshy back and big breasts. Under her armpits the sweat had made two dark half-moons. There was an animal eagerness in her movements. He continued to watch her. Then his lips curled in a twisted smile and he tapped on the door. She looked up. He beckoned to her to come into the room, which she did. He pulled her to the floor. In a few minutes it was all over, and he pressed a ten-rupee note into her hand. She took it and left.

Javed returned to his seat. God, how filthy she was, he said to himself. Then he held his head in his hands, stunned at what he had done. Why? He couldn't make it out. He sat there a long time, in the dark.

He was already in bed when Sophie returned. He was awake when she came into the bedroom, but he closed his eyes and pretended to be asleep. She quietly slipped into bed and in a few minutes was peacefully asleep. He lay awake for hours. What plans he had made for themselves for this night, their first wedding anniversary, and now he daren't even touch his wife. She was so close and yet so far.

The next day he fired Ram Kali. Sophie continued to be as beautiful as ever, if anything, even more beautiful when he thought of her in his imagination. But whenever he touched her, held her in a love embrace, a dark shadow would come between him and the woman he adored. In a way he felt he touched that beautiful vision, and yet, in another, he felt she was beyond his touch.

One morning, about six months after their wedding anniversary, he woke up early but did not get up. He lay in bed for almost an hour. He did not disturb Sophie. When she woke up, he said to her, 'You haven't had that dream for a long time?'

'What dream?' she asked.

'About Ram Kali.'

'Oh, that one, no. I told you it would go away. You shouldn't have fired her. How was she to blame?'

'The boatman is here,' announced one of the servants.

We were sitting, my sister Adiba and I, on the terrace at the back of the house. A hundred feet away and twenty feet below flowed the river, the Ganga, brimming and blue in the clear November afternoon. 'What a view!' I had exclaimed, when we sat down to a light lunch, soon after my arrival in Kherabad.

I had come to Kherabad primarily to discuss my wedding plans with my sister. I was getting married in December during the Christmas holidays, and my sister was to go in advance to our ancestral home in Agra to get things ready for the guests, mostly relatives, some of whom were coming from as far as Hydrabad Deccan, and to make the necessary arrangements for the *nikah* ceremony, the wedding feast and the music party.

Adiba's husband was the District Magistrate of Kherabad, hence the princely house with the choice location. From Kherabad I was going to Bhimsa, a village by the Ganga, in connection with some taxation problems that the Provincial Government was having with that *tehsil*. I was going there to see the *Tehsildar* of the region.

Hameed, Adiba's husband, had suggested that I should take the river route, which would be much nicer than a bus ride on a dusty road. The scenery, he said, was fantastic. We would pass the thickly wooded Jinga Hills and, finally, I could get some duck-hunting done along the way. I had jumped at the offer. He had arranged for the boat to come to the very doorsteps.

Hanif, the young servant boy, carried my bedding-roll—I was spending the night at the village—and a small hamper of food that my sister insisted I should take with me. We descended the river bank and I met Nathu, the boatman. He was a strong gentle man in his mid-thirties. Soon we were under way. We floated down the river, with Nathu plying the oars rhythmically at a leisurely pace. He was not very talkative, which suited me fine. I was enjoying the wind, the water, the blue sky, and above all my reverie of life with Razia, the girl I was about to marry.

I had met her at a party and had fallen head over heels in love with her. She grew to like me too after we had met a few times. Yes, she would marry me, she had said in answer to my inevitable query. But her parents put up a stiff resistance. I did not have a glamorous job and they were sure that their beautiful daughter would attract much better suitors. But when Razia firmly, though indirectly—that is through her mother—communicated to her father that she wanted to marry me, they gave in. And here I was looking at the world through the filter of her beauty.

'Those are not ducks?' I asked Nathu, pointing to some dark spots in the far distance on the white sand along the river.

'No, they are geese,' he said.

'Oh, I absolutely must have a crack at them,' I exclaimed, with the enthusiasm of the amateur sportsman.

'Okay. What you do is get behind that mound,' he said, pointing to a sand dune not far from where the geese were lying in the sun.

'Get off there,' he said, inclining his head toward a break in the river bank.

He took me there and I jumped out. Then ducking, crawling, dragging myself on my belly and carrying my gun in front of me, I made my way to the vantage point, behind which the geese were snoozing. As my head topped the curve of the sandy rise, the sentinel bird gave the alarm, and, as if released by a spring, the whole honking flock rose into the air. I too jumped to my feet and let go with both the barrels, dropping one bird. Excited and happy, I carried it back to the boat.

'Not bad! That's a fat bird,' said Nathu, and again we were on our way, gliding down the river.

After a couple of hours, Nathu said, more to himself than to me, 'I don't like it.'

'You don't like what?' I queried him.

'That black cloud over there,' he said. To my eyes it was no more than a little grey stain on the horizon.

'It's a storm cloud,' he said. 'I don't think we have more than half an hour to find a shelter.' And he increased the pace of his rowing.

'I know a place not far from here, an arm of the river that goes into those hills. I'll be able to make it there,' he said. The hills were at quite some distance, but then, he was rowing quickly.

Soon enough little rags of wind blew past us. The little speck we had seen on the horizon was now moving over us like a giant grey sliding roof. The wind turned to squalls and the first big drops of rain fell on our heads as Nathu left the river and entered a narrow creek.

We had an umbrella of trees arching over us now and the rain was only lightly filtering through the green canopy. As the clouds raced overhead, it quickly grew much darker. We rowed about half a mile inland up the narrow tributary, penetrating the thick vegetation.

We stopped near what was a crudely constructed cottage, abandoned now, a part of which had fallen in. There were no doors in the doorways and the shutterless windows were open squares in the bare walls. We hauled our things in. Inside, the shack was not as bad as it appeared from the outside. It would protect us from the weather well enough.

'I'm afraid we'll have to spend the night here,' said Nathu. 'It's not going to clear up in a hurry.'

'That's all right,' I said. I was not at all put about by the inconvenience.

We made a fire, had our supper, and, as it was quite dark now, we lay down to sleep. It hadn't really rained a great deal, but the wind and the lightning were truly terrible.

'You found a great spot for a night like this,' I said to Nathu.

'Oh, I have spent many nights here,' he replied, and then added, 'I had better build a fire to last us through the night. It will keep the wild animals away. We are inside the Jinga Hills, miles away from the nearest village.' He got up and added to the fire and lay down again. Soon we were fast asleep.

It must have been about three o'clock in the morning when my sleep was broken by the sound of someone laughing outside. It was a woman's laugh, musical like silver bells. I got up and went to the shutterless window to see who it was.

There was mottled moonlight outside—the trees near the cottage were not close set—and the ground looked like a carpet of light and grey patches. I looked up. The sky, all that I could see, was crystal clear. The storm had blown over and the moon was shining in its splendour, full and bright, almost like the day. In the lighted patches things were perfectly visible, and even in the shade under the trees visibility was not bad. But I saw no one. Who could have been laughing?

Then I saw her, a young woman, her form silvery like the moon even in the shade. She was dressed from the shoulders to the knees in an almost transparent length of muslin that was floating rather than fitted around her body. She was playfully running about and giving out little musical peals of laughter while she was being pursued by a young man, who was strong and brown like the earth, and who was wearing a dhoti that covered him from his waist to his calves. He was trying to catch her, but she eluded his grasp by dodging behind trees or escaping to the other side of the puddles that the rain water had formed, and emitting those silvery peels.

They played this game for a while and he eventually caught her. He held her in his embrace and she playfully went on resisting him, throwing her head back and laughing laughing all the time, till they tumbled to the ground and rolled on the grass, where he victoriously kissed her.

She lay in his arms for some time. Then they sat up and, holding hands, leaned their backs against a tree. What they said to each other I could not hear.

After a while they got up, strolled towards a swing that was suspended from a tall tree and got up on it. They sat side by side on its wooden seat, each with an arm behind the other as they grasped the ropes. Then they pushed off and started pumping the swing with their feet. Going back and forth the swing rose higher and higher till it was almost parallel to the ground at its highest points. As they shot up and swept down in that wide arc and the wind whistled through her hair, the woman again let out her musical shrieks of pleasure.

After some time they slowed down, stopped and got off. They were quiet now, and arm in arm walked in their bare feet through the puddles of rain water and, finally, disappeared under the trees.

I remained watching at my station for a long time, waiting for them to come back, but they did not. I rubbed my eyes. Was it a vision? Did I really see them or was I dreaming? I looked down at my rolled-out bedding. Yes, it was there. I looked at Nathu. He lay sound asleep. The fire had gone out, but the thought of the wild animals did not even cross my mind. I lay down happy and went back to sleep.

'*Babu*, wake up!' Nathu was saying. I opened my eyes; it was broad daylight. I got up, rolled up my bedding and got dressed. Nathu made a fire and boiled some water. We made tea and had our breakfast.

'The fire went out in the night,' he said.

'Yes, I saw it when I got up sometime after midnight. I was awakened by some sounds that I heard,' I said.

A worried look came over his face and he asked, 'It wasn't a tiger or a bear?'

'No, no, it wasn't a tiger or a bear. In fact, I am not even sure if I got up at all. Maybe it was all a dream.' I told him what I had seen, or what I believed I had seen. He listened intently to my story, not interrupting even once, and all the time a quiet smile played upon his simple peasant's face.

'Are you in love?' he asked when I had finished.

'Why, was it a lover's dream?'

'No, it was not a dream,' he said. 'What you saw was there all right; but only those who are in love can see it. I know some other people who have seen them. But I myself never have, although I have spent many nights here. But perhaps I didn't love the woman I married in the playful and moonlight kind of way that you saw.' And he told me about his wife, saying, 'Jasho was a fisherman's daughter. I am a fisherman. She was strong and as good as myself at casting the net and hauling in the catch. We are partners in water. Perhaps that's not love for Ramu and Rani.'

'Who are Ramu and Rani?' I asked.

'The man and woman you saw last night,' he replied.

'Do they live here?' I asked.

'No, they died long ago,' he said.

'What!' I exclaimed.

'I'll tell you about them when we get back on the river.'

We packed up, put out the fire, loaded our things onto the boat and worked our way through the tunnel of lush greenery. When we emerged on the vast expanse of the river, the water was glimmering in the gorgeous morning light. We resumed our journey and Nathu told me about the moon-coloured woman and the earth-coloured man.

'About fifty miles down the river, well beyond the cluster of the wild Jinga Hills, in which we have spent the night, is a village called Premabad. It was there that Rani's father lived long ago. He was almost like a king to the villagers; he was the top *zamindar*, owner of almost all the land in and around the village. He lived in a *haveli*, a big house, surrounded by his wealth and his beautiful family, of whom the most beautiful was his youngest child, a girl who went by the name of Rani or 'the queen'.

'Apart from his wealth and rank that earned him honour and respect, there was his high caste too. He was a Brahmin. But he was not a fanatic. With the exception of his cook, who was always a Brahmin, most of his servants were from the lower castes. And the man who looked after his cows was indeed of the *shudra* caste, from the so-called 'untouchables'. But everybody touched Ghasita, the cowherd, and he was in and out of the *haveli* all the time.

'Ramu was Ghasita's son and from his childhood he was Rani's playmate. The two of them romped together in the fields, chased the cows and played together all the time. No one minded it, that is, as long as they were children. But when Rani was fifteen, restrictions were imposed.

'Soon she would be married, she was told, and go to her husband's home and assume responsibility of a whole household as a grown woman. It was not good for her to be seen in the company of a boy, and a *shudra* boy at that. People talk and say all kinds of malicious things. Now that she was of a marriageable age she should exercise more prudence.

'Ramu was flatly ordered not to seek Rani's company. In fact, he was not to come into the *haveli* at all. However, he was often in the nearby cowsheds, assisting his father. And it was there that they secretly would meet, Rani and he. She would quietly steal into one of the little barns where he would be waiting for her.

'The family, secure in their aristocratic superiority, could not even imagine that the two lovers were still meeting. It was only when Rani's mother went by chance into one of the sheds that she saw them sitting in a corner holding hands.

'The *zamindar* was furious. He called the girl up to his room and shouted at her. Where was her shame? She was playing with filth. She was not thinking of the family's honour, not even of her own future. He told her that he had ordered Ramu to be sent to another village where he would live with his uncle. If he ever came back, and if the two of them were seen together again, he would simply have him beaten to death.

'The next day Ramu was gone. Ghasita was treated with greater care than before, but he could not look anyone in the eye. The guilt of his son made him feel guilty too, and he moved like one who was trying to be invisible. And if the *zamindar* spoke a kind word to him, which he sometimes did, he would immediately stoop down and touch his feet.

'"You are mother and father to us, lord," he would say, with tears of gratitude showing in his eyes and the demon of fear gripping his heart.

'The *zamindar* also earnestly embarked on finding a match for his daughter, who herself was now very quiet and withdrawn. She did not protest; she did nothing either to oppose or support what he was doing. Her father liked to think that she had dutifully submitted to his will, but in his heart of hearts he was not really convinced.

'He didn't have to try very hard to find a mate for Rani. There were so many young men wanting to marry this beautiful and wealthy girl; proposals poured in.

'Finally, a match was decided upon. Rani would go to Pritamgarh as the daughter-in-law, not of a *zamindar* like her father, but of the Rajah of Pritamgarh. The father and mother were elated at the prospect. They did not name her Rani for nothing, her mother said; she was destined to be a queen.

'As the wedding date approached, Rani sank deeper into silence and dejection. Her usually lively and cheerful face was now habitually melancholy and pensive. Her mother and father and brothers tried to cheer her up. Girls get married, they said; they have to leave the homes of their childhood. Certainly, she would be separated from those she had lived with and loved all her life, and who on their part had doted on her. But she would have an equally good home now and lots and lots of love from her husband and the people she was going to.

'They never talked of Ramu. They, in fact, would have been surprised if somebody had told them what the cause of her grief was, so deeply into the dark depths of their minds had they thrust the idea of a liking existing between a Brahmin girl and a *shudra* boy.

'The wedding day arrived. Rani had not eaten, or

106

had eaten next to nothing, for a whole week, and when one of her maids went to her bedroom to awaken her and begin preparing the bride for the evening ceremony—the bridegroom's party was arriving in the afternoon—she came out howling and sobbing. Rani was dead.

'The whole household was thrown into a commotion. The mother beat her breast and tore her hair. The father moaned and cried and said why did he live to see this day?

'The news of the *zamindar*'s daughter's death on her wedding day spread like wildfire in the village and beyond. A man was rushed to Pritamgarh to inform the bridegroom's party of the tragedy that had struck before they started. By noon people from far and near were pouring in to comfort the *zamindar* in his bereavement.

'In another part of the house preparations were under way to take the body to the cremation ghat for burning.

'Evening had fallen by the time the pundits had finished the religious rituals, chanted the prayers, and got the bier ready. Rani's body was wrapped in a white shroud and was placed on a long narrow frame made of two bamboos joined firmly together by a number of crosssticks. It was heaped high with flowers. Two men, one in front, the other behind, lifted the light bier on to their shoulders, and the sad procession started out. Crying *'Ram nam sat hai'* they slowly wound their way towards the river.

'It was completely dark when they reached the cremation ghat. The sky was overcast and a few drops of rain began to fall. The priests proceeded with the last ceremony. They arranged the fire logs many layers deep, into a funeral pyre, lavishly poured ghee over it, and placed the body on top of the pile. The mother and father uttered heart-rending shrieks, and then the mother collapsed, falling to the ground, where she kept banging her head. Loving hands helped her up.

'Finally, the funeral pyre was torched. It was at that precise moment that the rain came pouring down. The flames fed with fat were rising and trying to establish themselves, and the rain, now falling in sheets, was dousing them. Then the whole world lit up as a huge ball of lightning hit the ground yards away from the mourners, followed by a deafening crash of thunder that sent waves of terror through them. And when the roaring thunder hurled another immense fire-ball, and this time in their very midst, the crowd stampeded. Everybody ran. The older, fatter ladies of the *haveli*, who could not run, had to be lifted up and carried by the servants, as everybody headed for home. They ran, and as they ran they looked back and saw more balls of fire bouncing on the burning ghat. The thunder pursued them and they ran harder.

'The storm was as short as it was violent. When it was over, there was not a soul near the dead body except a young man who was standing near the now cold funeral pyre. The rain drenched him to the skin, but he was oblivious to it; he was drowning in grief. The fire on the *chita* had gone out, but he was burning inside.

'The rain had stopped, the lightning and thunder were gone, and the wind had died down. Everything was quiet and the young man stood like a statue, when he heard a groan and saw a movement inside the winding sheet.

'Like a wild animal he jumped onto the pyre and began to tear off the partly singed and completely soaked shroud. Rani sat up and opened her eyes.

'Where are we?' she said.

'"It's all right; it's all right,' he kept repeating as he extricated her from the winding sheet, lifted her off the log pile, and set her down on the ground. She stood there, naked, by his side. He flung away the torn cloth of the dead, took off his *kurta* and put it on her.

'Then they started walking, away from the ghat, away from the village, along the river bank, towards the distant Jinga Hills. And they talked. Ramu told her what had happened. Probably, he said, she had the disease that he once heard old Vedji talk about in which heartbeat and breathing are almost gone as is the heat of the body. They thought she was dead and brought her to the cremation ground. And then about the fearsome thunder and lightning and how everybody ran.

'She asked him where he had come from. He told her he had heard of her death and had come to the village. He was there around noon, but he did not go in; he hung around at the outskirts. Later on, when the funeral procession started, he had followed it at a distance, keeping out of sight. And then at the burning ghat he watched from a distance, standing behind a tree. And when everyone had gone, he had come out and had been standing there ever since.

'They kept walking, hand in hand. They walked all night.

'The next morning the *zamindar* returned to the site with his priests to complete the unfinished rites, and they were all very surprised to find the body gone. They found the shroud. It had been torn, and there were some blood stains on it. They concluded that wild animals had taken away the body. They grieved some more and went home.

'It was years later that reports began to circulate that a young couple lived in the dangerous forest of the Jinga Hills. They were also sighted a few times on the bank of the river. But they never stayed for more than a fleeting glimpse. And then the story was slowly pieced together as to who they were.'

'Some believe,' Nathu concluded, 'that they are still alive. But that cannot be. They came here more than a hundred years ago.'

When he had finished his story, I emerged from a sort of trance, and all I could think of saying was, 'So you never saw them?'

'No,' he said. 'I told you my wife and I are partners in water, not players in the moonlight.'

I smiled at his simple answer, but in the dim and dreaming part of my mind I saw a moonlike face that was Razia's.

STOMACH-ACHE : A PROSE FABLIAU

Lala Manohar Lal Agarwal's sexual problem in his brand new marriage was of a geometrical nature. He was himself like a huge balloon, whereas his bride Soni was like a pair of compasses with stiff legs that would open only this much and no more. How to fit the balloon between the legs of the instrument in such a way that the nozzle of the big sphere would touch the vertex of the compasses' angle was the task set for him on his wedding night. He tried again and again to establish the contact, but to no avail. When he had failed repeatedly, he attempted the hope strategy. That is, he closed his eyes, noisily breathed out, drew his tummy in, or at least he thought he had done so, and imagining that he was now sufficiently deflated, quietly tried to sneak in. But the trick didn't work. In his desperation he even resorted to force, and tried to distend his wife's legs to an angle of 180°. But Soni was not a rag doll. Quite the contrary, she was a superbly-formed athlete with long and well-toned muscles and joints that were springy with a steel firmness, and were not held together by rubber bands.

It was indeed the girl's athleticism that had caught the eye and attention of Manohar's father, the big *Seth*, Lala Hira Lal Agarwal, and had made him decide on the spot that his son would marry this girl.

The Agarwals were *banyas*, the well-known trading caste of India, whose affluence and obesity is legendary. It may be pointed out, in the interest of fairness and objectivity, that not all *banyas* are rich and rotund. Like any other social stereotype, this one too has its exceptions, and there are some members of this class who are both slim and badly off. But the Agarwals were not among the exceptions. They had been, from generation to generation, fabulously rich and notoriously fat. Manohar's grandfather, for example, is still remembered in Ghaziabad as the fattest man that that town has ever produced.

All his life he had sat in his textile store from dawn till dusk, moving everybody around him, but not stirring himself. He had, in this way, amassed a huge fortune and also an equal amount of blubber. By the time he reached middle age, he had grown to such enormous proportions that some areas of his body extended beyond his reach; he could not scratch himself, and it became impossible for him to have a proper bath by himself. The arrangement that he had made in this connection was that every morning, four of his most stalwart domestics took him out to a creek on the outskirts of the town, sat him in the water, and gave him a thorough scrubbing. They laved his back, washed his limbs, and finally went to work on his monumental belly, which consisted of rolls upon massive rolls of fat. They parted the folds, inserted an oversize towel edgewise in the opening and then pulled it from side to side, like two loggers sawing down a tree.

When all the tummy folds had been treated in this fashion and the daily deposit of grime and grease removed, Lalaji felt and smelled clean for the rest of the day, except for one evening when he started exuding strong whiffs of a putrid smell.

The servants were hurriedly summoned to see what was the matter. They went over his whole body with their noses like hounds trying to pick up a scent, but could not locate the source of the foul odour until they came to one of the stomach folds. When they lifted it, they found compressed in it a dead fish, which apparently had become trapped in the course of the morning ablution, and had now begun to decompose.

Manohar's own father was a shrewd and far-sighted man. Not only did he plan to increase the family fortune, which any Agarwal would have done, but he also resolved to decrease the family girth, at least of the future generations. In pursuance of the first, that is, the monetary goal, he opened a new store in Delhi, which is a stone's throw from Ghaziabad. He moved to the big city himself to look after the new business, leaving the old one in the hands of his two sons. Concerning the second objective, he was determined to marry his sons outside his chubby community in order to improve the family heredity. And as luck would have it, an opportunity came along which he seized immediately.

He had gone one summer morning to a village in the neighbouring countryside to inspect his landholdings there, and was standing in the middle of a field with some of his agricultural tenants when he saw Soni. The peasant girl was driving a small herd of goats to pasture, when one of the frisky beasts broke away from the pack and took off like a deer. And there was Soni speeding after it in hot pursuit, racing like an antelope herself.

When the delinquent had been rounded up, Seth Hari Lal had the girl brought to him, and there she was, standing before him, her golden face glowing after the sprint. She was dressed in a single length of rough, earth-coloured cloth. The middle of her one-piece garment was tightly wound around her spare waist. Its upper half ran up and across her back and draped only one shoulder, leaving the other one exposed in its sculptured beauty; then coming down in front, it concealed and contoured her firm and pointed breasts, and was finally tucked into the waistband. The lower half of her simple dress covered her middle, tightly going round and outlining her strong and slightly protruding hips, and then fell in a flare to a little below her knees. Her beautifully-shaped calves and feet were bare. There was not an ounce of fat to be seen on her body.

Sethji asked who she was. He was informed that she was Rupa's daughter. Rupa was one of his minor tenants. Hira Lal decided then and there that this seventeen-year-old was going to be one of his daughters-in-law.

The villagers could not believe their good fortune when the coming wedding was announced. Their own Soni was going to be a *Sethani*, a millionaire's wife. The *banya* community objected vehemently because of the girl's lower caste. But Hira Lal was not to be deterred by the outcry. A man weighing the heavy future of his family is not easily swayed by such light considerations as tradition and the past. Hira Lal wanted to make sure that none of his grandsons fished with their tummies.

This was how Manohar came to marry Soni and was

presented with a geometrical problem that he could not solve on his wedding night, nor in the nights that followed.

In a couple of months after Hira Lal had executed his bold decision, he passed away. He was fine in the morning but was gone in the evening. His overworked heart could not take the strain any more, so it simply decided to stop beating.

Being the eldest, Manohar had to rush to Delhi to take charge of the big store there, leaving the smaller one in Ghaziabad under the supervision of his younger brother. He did not take Soni with him.

However, he made it a point to come home every weekend to be with his wife. But every time he went back frustrated, and in a few months even the routine visits stopped; now he came only when an urgent family or business matter required his presence. He was not unhappy in Delhi for his sexual devil was not of the tormenting type. Besides, his financial angel kept him elated and excited: business was booming as never before.

But life in Ghaziabad for poor Soni was not much fun. True, she had money, respect, a fine home, and an army of servants, but she was not happy. The only thing that interested her in her new surroundings was the kitchen garden in the backyard of the palatial house. The 'vegetable patch', as it was called, was a walled-in area the size of two tennis courts, and it was lush with plants and creepers. She spent hours there every day watering, hoeing, and pruning the plants, training creepers up the walls, or just pottering about in the greenery. It reminded her of her former life and gave her great satisfaction. And whenever the mood took her, which was not infrequently, she had her swiftest mare harnessed to a light gig and raced off to her village, where she spent the day with her family and saw old friends, especially Mohini, a childhood chum and a young widow, who had turned to religion.

Being a widow, Mohini soon found out that she had been completely cut off from the pleasures of the secular world. Marrying again was, of course, out of the question. She could not, poor thing, even join her friends in such innocent fun as singing or dancing or dressing up and going to parties, even on such occasions as *holi* and *divali*. Barred from the delights of the senses, she had turned to the spiritual world to see if it held any comforts for her.

The two friends talked to each other of their plights, and Soni, though not a widow, but almost, began to incline toward religion too. She even visited a holy man whom Mohini had mentioned, and who had renounced the world and now lived a hermit's life in the deep recesses of a wood, some five or six miles from their village.

Soni made a detour one afternoon when returning to town and met the recluse. He was in his middle age. His hair was iron grey, his beard grizzled, and his body, most of which was naked, was covered in ash. His face had a peaceful expression and his eyes had a distant but peaceful look. He showed her round and finally took her to his little temple, a small and dark prayer room. When the door opened, she thought she was looking at a corner of the night sky glimmering with stars: little earthenware lamps with tiny flames filled the niches on the back wall of the windowless sanctum. Both of them went in and sat down on the floor. As her eyes became accustomed to the dim light, she could make out little figures—garlanded statuettes of gods and goddesses—ranged on a ledge. The holy

116

man meditated in silence for a few minutes and then broke into song, singing devotional songs of long ago—Mira Bai's *bhajans*. The insinuating music, the heavy smell of burning incense, the semi-darkness of the little chamber filled her mind with an ecstatic peace. It was a new experience for her and she liked it so much that in the next few days she had a replica of the hermit's cell constructed in her house.

Every morning she sat and sang there, and when the new-found feeling came, she felt that she was an inhabitant of a hot country, awakening uneasily in the heat of the night. And then, during this discomfort, a cool breeze would begin to blow over her from a distant unearthly shore of the night. It was a total mood that permeated her whole being, and while it lasted nothing else mattered.

But there was another total mood also. This one occurred when she actually awoke in the heat of the night and there was no cooling breeze, only hot throbs rising from the earth and passing through her and filling her whole being with unease and yearning. Her entire young body ached and she wanted to hold another body in her passionate embrace so tightly that her sinews would break and she would die.

The next time she drove to the hermit's hideaway, he was not to be seen anywhere, until her servant spotted him a few hundred yards away from his dwelling. He was working with a lad in a little field by the side of a stream. She joined them.

'This is where we grow our food,' he said, and introduced her to the lad, a boy of fourteen or fifteen. The boy was dressed only in a loin-cloth; his upper body and legs were bare. He was strongly built, but his most striking feature was an air of virginal purity that surrounded him. You could see the purity in the texture of his skin, in the clearness of his eyes, and in the morning freshness of his face. She talked to him and he blushed. She was immediately attracted by his innocent shyness, the shyness of the young that hides from its owner and reveals to the viewer the human treasures, both light and dark, that lie concealed behind the confusion.

The hermit had told her that Madho was his son.

'I did not know you had a son,' she resumed.

'Yes, I do,' he said automatically, and then added more thoughtfully, 'In fact, I am here because of him.' She did not follow his meaning and looked at him enquiringly. He elaborated, 'His mother died giving birth. I was completely devastated. I lost the will to live. I tried but I could not pick up the pieces again. So, after a few months, I picked up my son and walked away and said goodbye to the world. I have been here ever since, now over fourteen years.' She was listening attentively, and he continued, 'I'm glad for myself that I came here. I found Bhagwan. But I wasn't sure then and I'm not sure now whether I was fair to the boy. I was a bad mother to him, and I don't think I have been a good teacher. All he knows about are gods and plants, nothing about people and the world. We haven't been among people, to a village or a city, more than a dozen times in all these years. Now I am trying to persuade my brother in Delhi to take in my son. He has four of his own. He can apprentice him to a trade.'

They talked for an hour. In the end Soni made him an offer. Madho could work as her gardener and look after her prayer room to begin with, and if an opportunity arose she would help him. She'd keep her eyes open. The hermit readily closed the deal.

So there was Madho in Ghaziabad, running like a puppy after his young mistress, working with her in the garden, lighting lamps in the little temple and joining her in her devotional songs. She liked him in both these contexts, physical and spiritual, more so in the former. She liked to touch him, and did so openly, barely concealing her pleasure, as they worked or prayed together, and she encouraged him to touch her too. But he never took the hint. No mysterious gleam ever narrowed his eyes, no crooked smile distorted his lips. His innocence was too dense.

She had to go farther. So one day, as they were working in the garden together, she threw up her arms with a girlish shriek and let her sari drop from her shoulder, and said to him, 'See if there is an insect inside the back of my blouse.' He put his hand in and searched for the vermin all over, high and low.

'No, there isn't; it must have fallen out,' he said, with the honesty of a child.

She gave him more and more liberties with her body, but could not get the desired response.

'Doesn't he know anything about sex at all?' she said to herself.

Then one day she strolled into her bedroom with him at her heels and said to him, 'Madho, I have a stomach-ache.'

He looked concerned and said, 'Shall I run over to Vedji's drugstore and get some *churan* powder for you?'

'No, that won't be necessary,' she said. 'What I need, I think, is a good massage. Would you give my tummy a rub?' Of course, he would, he said.

She lay down on the bed, unbuttoned her blouse and pushed her sari down a little. He massaged her belly.

'Is it better?' he asked after some time.

'No,' she said, 'I don't think we are getting to the root of the pain. It's deeper down.' He didn't know what to do. She removed her sari altogether and said, 'See if there is a way of getting in.' Yes, he found a way all right and tried the digital probe.

'That's better,' she said, 'but you are falling short.' What was he to do?

'Try this,' she said, stroking the front of his dhoti, which had mysteriously risen, 'it might go farther.' He tried. It did go farther.

'You are almost there,' she said. He tried harder. But somehow the pain got worse, or so it seemed to him, for now she began to heave and writhe. It took all he had to stay on top of the rising pain, but in the end he was able to wrestle it down.

When it was all over, he looked down at her. She was smiling.

'It's all right now,' she said. He was glad that he had been of some little service to his mistress in her distress.

She now had the attack almost every day, and Madho was ever ready to run to her aid. After a time he became such an expert that he could detect the symptoms of the ache without her telling him, and, in fact, sometimes even before she herself had become aware of them.

Months passed, very quickly.

Towards the end of the ninth month she wrote to her husband that she was shortly going to have a baby. Manohar Lal was greatly surprised. He did not remember his marriage being consummated. All he had been able to do was to sprinkle his wife from above. But then, he thought, it didn't take much for a woman to get pregnant. Even if a drop trickled in, the right way, that would do the trick. After all, Father Sky impregnated Mother Earth like that, letting out all sorts of noises from his orifices and coming off before he had grasped her. That put his mind to rest. He was also glad that he would now have an heir and not have to worry about marrying again for that purpose. Of course this time he would have gone for a girl from his own community, a soft-fleshed, loose-jointed woman whose legs would fold upwards along her sides until the feet touched the ears.

In a few days he arrived in Ghaziabad and preparations to celebrate the happy event got under way. The town park next to his residence was commandeered; mammoth tents were erected; the grounds were covered over with plush carpets; and multitudes of little coloured lights decorated the tents inside and out. He also called in the best caterers in town and ordered tons of *puris, parathas*, spicy vegetables, and sweetmeats of all kinds.

When the news was announced that a son had been born to the Seth, the celebration broke like a storm. There were fireworks, music, dancing, and feasting day after day for a whole week. The rich and the poor, almost the whole town, had been invited to the festivities.

When the week-long orgy of eating and drinking was finally over, many a stomach began to rumble and grumble, including Lala Manohar's. The next morning it got so bad that he had to go to his room and lie down. And when he saw Madho go by, he called out to him and said, 'Go to Vedji's drugstore and get me some *churan* powder. I have a bad stomach-ache.'

'That won't be necessary,' said the boy, 'I know how to cure it. As a matter of fact, Sethaniji used to get it almost every day, and I fixed it in no time.'

'Oh!' said Manohar.

'You just lie down on the floor, on your tummy,' said the boy. Manohar did what he had been asked to do. The boy expertly removed his dhoti.

'What are you doing?' Lalaji shouted.

'You just wait and see,' said the lad. As the cure began, rather suddenly, Manohar fought and resisted, but to no use. Hoisted on his prodigious tummy, he was as helpless as a turtle lying on its back. He waved his arms and legs like one swimming in the air, but he was unable to turn over.

When it was all over, he felt terribly humiliated, shocked and scandalized. But no matter what, the truth must be stated: his stomach-ache was gone.

THE CUSTARD-APPLE HUNT

Rising with the dawn, the four children would disappear before the rest of the family was up. It would not even be properly light when some invisible conspirator whispered in their ears to get up. They awoke and quietly slipped out of their beds, armed themselves with the slender bamboo poles that supported their mosquito nets, and stole away without disturbing the elders. Soon they were lost among the shrubs and the trees and the hunt was on.

Half an hour later, when the sun was slanting bright rays across the sky, their mother got up—late as usual— for her morning prayers. She looked at the four empty beds with the collapsed mosquito curtains and muttered to herself, 'Mad creatures!' Then arranging her *dopatta* over her head and around her shoulders, she walked to the front door, turned the key in the lock, and went into the house. She threw open all the doors and windows that had been fastened against the night. In a short while, the servant would come and sweep out the rooms.

By now the children were far afield in their search

for custard apples. On the grounds of their own house there were a few custard-apple trees, but they had been picked clean, so the young hunters were venturing into new territories, such as the compounds of the neighbours, the High School, and even the Christian cemetery in which there were as many trees as graves. They had opened their campaign ten days ago, when Jamil, by chance, had spied a plump custard apple peeping out from a cluster of leaves. The sight of it had electrified him and had sent him bolting into the house to fetch a bamboo stick to knock it down. He and the three younger children had the time of their lives landing it.

Once secured, it was duly treated with lime from mother's *pandan*, for Jamil, in the infinite wisdom of his eleven years, knew that to ripen a custard apple you have to break off the stalk, daub the scar with moist lime, and pack it away amongst clothes and things to keep it warm. In a few days, it would turn yellow and be ready for eating.

Having done all this and, lodging it safely among his clothes in his own trunk, he had led the search for fresh ones. And now there were three more pairs of young eyes to spot the prey, and the owner of the youngest pair was only five-years-old, a girl.

The four children would disappear at daybreak and would not even return for breakfast, so completely had the search captured their imagination. A servant would be sent to bring them back, and they would come slinking in like thieves, their faces glowing from the exertion in the pure morning air, with traces of dry perspiration showing on their cheeks. If mother was in the kitchen then it was all right. And on most mornings she was there, in spite of Nihal Sahib's injunction to the contrary. She had borne her husband twelve children and the old gentleman realized that she was worn out and needed rest, so she was not to go and work unnecessarily in the kitchen. But every morning when the warm smell of spices and frying fats wafted from the kitchen to her nostrils, she could not resist the temptation to be there herself.

If she happened to be in the dining room, the youngsters would not lift their eyes. She scolded them and told them that she would break their legs if they went out again. But she never did break their legs; she had always been loving and kind to her children.

The youngsters were very happy, enjoying themselves, when, without warning, the storm broke over their heads. One day the neighbour's servant was seen in conversation with Nihal Sahib. He had brought a complaint from his master: the children were plundering his trees. If they wanted custard apples they should come to him, he said, and ask him for them. Instead, they were ruining the trees. That very morning he had seen them, and when he had come out shouting, the young poachers had run away, making good their escape.

When the servant had left after delivering the message, Nihal Sahib was in an ugly mood. Something in the message had stung him—his children asking for custard apples from that man! He shouted for Jamil; his temper was rising and his voice unsteady. The moment the boy appeared he flew at him, slipper in hand, shouting, 'You swine, why did you go there?' And before the frightened child could form an answer, he struck him twice in the face with the slipper. Jamil covered his face with his arms to ward off further blows and burst out crying, saying he had not gone anywhere. This brought on a shower of blows on the head and the covering hands. 'You dare lie to me,' shrieked his father, beside himself with rage.

Aslam, Nihal Sahib's eldest son, a man of twenty-six, was sitting at the other end of the verandah reading a book. He had been there all morning, had seen the scampering children when the neighbour had come after them, and had seen that they were only three and that Jamil was not one of them. He had not accompanied them that day. It seemed inhuman to him that the boy should be beaten so brutally when he had not been there at all. He felt that his father seemed to take out his anger and frustration on Jamil most of the time. Noise in the house, knocking over of the furniture in the drawing room and other trivial occurrences would ruffle his temper and he would beat him, saying, 'It must be this mad one!'

In Aslam's mind this injustice on his father's part had begun to rankle. If he has to hit someone, why does he choose a defenceless child? And today he was beating the life out of him. A kind of fury gripped him and getting up he interfered, saying loudly, 'He did not go.'

This made his father jump at the crying child and strike him harder. Aslam's blood rushed to his face and, in a blinding fit of anger and excitement, he yelled at the top of his voice, 'He did not go. Do you hear?'

His father turned on him, his eyes blazing and his face distorted with anger. 'Shut up, he did!' he shouted shrilly.

Aslam shouted back, 'No, he did not.'

'Shut up, you insolent rascal. Is your father a liar?' he screamed, dancing with rage.

By now the whole household was in a commotion. The younger children had gone scurrying to places of safety like frightened rabbits. Aslam's sister swept him in her arms to his room saying, 'Brother, what are you doing?'

His mother dragged his father to another room, exclaiming, 'Oh, God! What has got into you? The older you get the more ill-tempered you become.'

The old man cried out, 'Now it's your turn. Hurl shoes at my head. What more is left? That mannerless scoundrel! I will not put up with this in my own house! I am not living on anyone's charity! I am not dependent on anyone! In my own house. . . .' Gradually the shouting died down, but every word of it had reached Aslam's ears.

The moment he was in his room, he experienced an overpowering sense of weakness, a complete hollowness inside. His knees grew feeble under him, unable to support his weight. His heart was beating rapidly, his mind was dizzy, and he was astonished at what he had done. The excitement of the incident had sustained him; the minute that was over all was over. He felt that his life was being drained out of him. The words from the other room had reached him and had wounded him deeply, all the more so because his defences were down now. He was being fired at when he was carrying away the dead from the battlefield. The words about dependence and money cast an agony in his soul as they had special meaning for him. 'How could he?' he repeated to himself in pain.

It was true he was working and independent now. But there were years of dependence even after college when no job came his way. And even now he was a poor schoolmaster, turning to home for help from time to time. He swore that he would never ask for a penny from them in future. But then, his father had been so solicitous and generous. Where were these feelings hiding? Why did he have to use such heavy guns against him? Tears began to fill his eyes and a painful lump hurt his throat.

An audible silence had fallen on the house. Everyone seemed to be moving on tiptoe as if a surgical operation were in progress there. The midday meal was completely quiet. Eyes avoided meeting. His father was not there. He usually ate by himself.

After the meal, Aslam again found himself alone in his room. He was feeling like a patient who had just come out of anaesthesia and time stretched like a grey endlessness before him. It was a mercy, he thought, that his school opened the next day and he would be leaving in the evening. It would have been unbearable to live like this for any length of time.

A little later his mother came into his room. They sat in silence for some time. Then she said, 'You should not have shouted at him. After all, he is your father ... he's grown ill-tempered.' Her voice faltered at times and her eyes grew moist. Then she asked him if he needed anything, if he had enough shirts.

A few hours later he was taking his leave. 'Go and see your father,' his mother said.

'No, mother,' he said quietly.

'Yes, you must. He is your father. Besides, it would be very painful for me if you two parted like this.' He went into his father's room and told him that he was going. His father answered with an inarticulate sound in his throat and the interview was over.

The children gathered round him, crying, 'Goodbye, brother,' and 'When will you come again?'

Rehana, his youngest sister, who was standing next

to him and barely came up to his waist, piped up, 'Every time you go you say you will send me sweetmeats, but you never do.'

He smiled, and putting his hand on her shoulder he drew her against his side and said, 'This time I'll send you a lot of sweets. That's a promise.'

There were more farewells and then he turned quickly and left. His mother was crying quietly and he feared that he would not be able to hold back his tears for long. So he escaped, giving them one more hasty glance, seeing the waving hands and hearing the confused good-byes.

As the train rushed along in the night, he thought of the fifteen-day holiday he had spent at home. The children had come to the station to receive him. They had always liked going to the station as one after another of their brothers and sisters came from their universities and colleges for the holidays. And when they were all together it was such fun. What stories they had to tell one another. And they never tired of talking. Sometimes, from lunch to tea time, they kept sitting at the dining table and the room rang with their chatter and laughter. After supper the session would continue for hours and then their mother would come and say, 'It's getting on for eleven. Father says aren't you going to sleep?'

It was not so good now as it used to be in the previous years. Two sisters had married and had gone to their homes. Two brothers had chosen their ruts in life and kept to them and did not find time to visit home regularly. But even then it was great fun and the schoolmaster always looked forward to his visits. Now he peered into the darkness outside and put his head out of the open train window into the cool of the night and thought, 'Will I come again?' A tear shivered on his eyelids and dropped, and then a few more.

Next day when mother rose, late as usual, for her morning prayers, the sun sent slanting bright rays across the sky. She looked at the four empty beds and the collapsed mosquito curtains and muttered to herself, 'Mad creatures!' Then arranging her *dopatta* over her head and around her shoulders, she unlocked the front door and went in.

A BICYCLE

The engines throbbed violently and the ferry pushed off. It was a fine morning, and in the blue waters of the Ganga the falling rays of the sun seemed to break and scatter.

'Move a bit, Kesho,' said an old worker, and Kesho shifted. The old man propped his bicycle against the ferry's wall and squeezed himself down next to the young man.

Once the hustle and bustle of the start was over the confusion of the workers' talk rose again on the air. There were about fifty of them, smoking and talking and spitting into the water, crossing over to the tannery on the opposite bank. The workers living in the eastern part of the city always used the company's ferry, the city bridge across the river being some five miles further up the stream.

Kesho was silent. He was thinking that there was one less mouth to feed now; his mother had died the previous week. He looked towards the burning-ghat in the distance; they had cremated her there. The foul smell of burning flesh seemed to fill his nostrils and he leaned forward and spat into the river. A tortoise rose to the surface and instantly dove down. His mother's illness and the funeral rites had left him badly off. In fact, he was in debt. But from now on he was determined to put by some money every month.

The thought infused a happy satisfaction in him. He listened to the steady chugging of the engines and watched the bicycle before him. How visibly the tremor of the ferry was passing through its frame! He turned to the old man next to him and said, '*Baba*, when did you buy that bicycle?'

'Oh, long ago, my boy, years back. Let me see. It's a little older than my youngest son and he is almost a man now.'

'Things were cheap in those days, weren't they?' Kesho asked.

'Oh, yes, they were,' the old man replied, 'very cheap. Those were the better days. You earned little, but it was enough. Money was worth something. I don't know what things are coming to, prices going through the ceiling. It will become impossible to live if things go on like this. This bicycle you see before you, how much do you think I paid for it? Only twenty-five rupees, mind you, tools and all. Now it must be double that price, I guess.'

'Double!' echoed Kesho. 'A Hercules costs well over a hundred rupees now.'

'*Hei Bhagwan*!' the old man exclaimed. 'Over a hundred rupees? A bicycle costing over a hundred rupees? Who can afford to buy a bicycle now?'

Kesho was silent for a while. A light of happy desire began to shine in his eyes until they looked like the waters of the Ganga in the morning sun. Then, with a little hesitation and blushing, he said, '*Baba*, I will buy a bicycle one day.'

'At that price!' the old man exclaimed. 'Not at that price! A hundred rupees is a lot of money. I should walk if I were you.'

And Kesho did continue to walk, for years and years. Each single pie that he could save he put by like a miser; even then the money did not seem to grow, unlike the price of a bicycle which kept mounting up. He denied himself and the family as much as he could. Four flat cakes of maize, a few chillies done to paste with some salt and occasionally some *dal* had been his midday and evening meal. He barely spent anything on his clothes. He had a raise or two, but with the prices going up and more children coming, he found it increasingly difficult to save even two or three rupees a month.

He had three children by now. He had resolved after each not to have any more. But after the day's work, when his limbs were tired and the children were asleep, his desire would wake up. Resolution had been so easy in the light of day, but in the quiet of the night it was different. 'It's my own weakness; it's my own fault,' he would chide himself. 'I will never be able to buy a bicycle like that. In ten years I have saved only two hundred rupees (by now the price of a bicycle had climbed to two hundred and fifty). I take a vow that I shall not touch Radha any more.' But he went on touching her, all the same.

'Kesho,' his wife said one day, 'you need only fifty rupees more, why don't you sell my bracelets? We can get them again.'

'Radha,' he said, becoming angry and genuinely so,

'don't talk to me like that. A bicycle is a toy to me. Am I to take away your ornaments for it? Besides, you brought them with you, your people gave them to you. Who am I to take them away from you?'

So a bicycle, in the heat of an argument and in the fatigue of the night was a toy to him. But not in the daytime when he was by himself. What had been a dream had now become a passion. Truly, from his childhood he had wanted a bicycle. But then the mere thought of it gave him pleasure. Now he must touch it, feel it, possess it. Every bicycle that passed him he noticed. Outside cinema houses he saw hundreds of them. He would stand there a long time, watching them. A thought would sometimes turn in his mind like a worm: one less out of so many wouldn't matter. 'No, no,' he would say, and brush away the thought with a movement of his hand and go away.

Five more years passed. Grey hairs had begun to appear on his temples, when one day he pocketed all his savings and set out to buy a bicycle, walking with the long measured strides of one who had walked all his life. In the store he spoke a few words and a Hercules bicycle was pumped up and handed to him.

'That will be . . . ' and before the dealer had concluded his sentence Kesho handed him the bills that he held in his perspiring palm. The dealer counted out three hundred and eleven rupees, looked up in surprise at the rustic figure before him and said, 'Why, it's the exact amount. How did you know?'

Kesho tried to answer, but his lips were trembling and he could not say a word.

'Why, what's wrong with the man?' said the dealer. Kesho hung down his head, quietly lifted the bicycle out of the shop and walked away without looking back. His cheeks were wet with tears of happiness.

When he reached home the whole impoverished colony came flocking round.

'Kesho has bought a bicycle,'

'It's new and shining,'

'Brother Kesho how much did it cost?'

There was such excitement. Kesho's heart was ready to burst with joy, yet he was ashamed as if he had done something wrong, something which made him different from the rest of them, living in the gutter.

He had experienced a similar feeling when he got his first pair of shoes. He had told his father of his intention and the old man had said, 'Look at him, he wants to buy a pair of shoes. Who ever has worn shoes in the family? He wants to waste money on shoes. Is the earth too hard for your tender feet?' His face had burned with shame. But still he was glad when he bought them. He wished that the old man were alive now.

Life for him became one unbroken round of pleasure. When he went out on his bike and the air streamed through his hair, the swift motion exhilarated him, and happiness would bubble up in him till he hardly knew how to contain it. Everything was the same—the roads, the trees, the people around—but from the bicycle they looked so different. He liked them all and they made him happy. He thought that if everybody had a bicycle how happy the world would be.

'Radha,' he said one day to his wife, 'I'll take you out on my bicycle.'

'Who, me?' she asked in wonder, 'but it would be so shameless. What will people say?'

'I won't take you out in the daytime,' he said, as confusion spread over his face at the very thought of people looking at him and his wife on the bicycle, and he added, 'we'll go out at night.'

'Imagine me on a bicycle!' she said laughing, but she was pleased.

At night, when the children had gone to bed, they came out. Everything was quiet and still. The stars hung like lamps in the clear sky. The road lay straight before them, and the road lights looked like a line of stars strung out beside them. Occasionally a car passed. They found a little mound by the roadside and, resting one foot on it, Kesho sat on the bicycle and asked Radha to get up on the carrier behind him. Her weight unsteadied him. With a lunge on the pedal he started forward. The bicycle swerved dangerously to one side, then to the other, and Radha gave a squeak of fright.

'Sit still, you silly,' he said, controlling the bicycle.

'I almost fell off,' she cried.

'Hold me. Why don't you hold me?' he said. She hung on to him.

Now the bicycle was steady. A whir rose from its wheels in the stillness, and one electric-light pole after another swept by with astonishing rapidity.

'Not so fast, Kesho. I feel afraid.'

'This is not fast,' he said with pride, 'I can go much faster. You should see me flying to work in the morning.'

'Kesho,' she said after a pause, 'you should not go fast. If you fell you would hurt yourself.'

'You talk silly,' he said,. 'Who wants to fall? I don't want to break my bicycle.'

In the silence of the night they went on like this,

talking foolishly, happily and intimately. He took her to the Ganga, showed her the lights of his tannery on the other side, showed her his ferry that blotted the darkness a few shades deeper. The waves of the river washed softly on the shore and somewhere in a temple a bell was sounding dolefully.

When they returned, Radha said, 'It was very nice, Kesho,' and Kesho took her in his arms.

Six months went by and Kesho kept his bicycle as good as new. Then the rains set in. Almost every day there were clouds in the sky and the roads were wet and slushy, and in spite of his best care a couple of tiny rust stains appeared on one of the tire rims. He didn't like the rains.

The next morning as he set out for work the weather looked worse than usual. There was a blustering wind and thick black clouds were rolling in from the east like herds of wild elephants shaking their heads. He fought his way against the wind till he reached the river. He dismounted and wheeled his bicycle onto the ferry, rested it against its side and sat down.

'Hurry up, fellows,' shouted the Captain, 'we are already behind time and they don't like it over there if we are late.' A few workers were still standing on the shore. They came aboard.

The engines snorted and the shore receded. Kesho looked at the river and did not like its unfriendly swagger. It was turning and twisting too much and hit the boat like solid blocks rather than liquid waves. Within ten days, he thought, it would break its banks and spread over the countryside for miles and miles.

Suddenly, there was a terrific crash of thunder, followed by blinding rain, and the wind grew to gale force.

The little ferry was in trouble; it rose and plunged, pitched and rolled. All eyes were now on the hostile current. Then there went up a howl of despair. The boat shipped a huge wave, spun violently and capsized. Some of the men jumped overboard; the others went down with the ferry. The swirling, seething mass of water swallowed them all. Then some rose to the surface, battling desperately with the raging waves. Twenty-two of the fifty or so workers fought successfully to the shore; the rest were lost.

A few feeble and ill-equipped attempts were made at rescue, but to no effect. The raging elements were too much for little row boats trying to go in. In an hour or so the storm blew over, the police arrived, and a regular search for the lost was started. The river was dragged for miles. After hours of hard work, fifteen bodies were reclaimed; the others had been swept away by the strong current. It was decided that no more useful purpose would be served by continuing the search; so it was abandoned.

The recovered bodies lay on the sand, below the tannery wall, and the police cordoned off that area from the general public, giving access only to the tannery people and, of course, later on to the relatives of the deceased.

Two workers came that way and stood for some time looking at the dead men. One of them recognized his friend and said in shocked tones, 'Oh, that's Kesho over there.' And sure enough, it was Kesho, lying fifth from the left. Lying by his side was his bicycle, and he was attached to it with grips of steel.

A PROMISE TO KEEP

It was a blazing May afternoon and the wind, striking his face, seemed to come out of an oven. Nasim, sick with anxiety, hurried his steps towards the examination hall. At times he ran. The street was deserted, and, with the exception of the Students' Café, the shutters of the shops were up. The dust blew and whirled up in the road. With narrowed eyes he looked towards the University tower clock in the distance. Five minutes more. At three the bell would sound and the exam start. It was silly of him to have dozed off like that. He had been reading, had rested his head on the book, and when he awoke it was eight minutes to three. He had grabbed his pen and notes and flung himself out of the room, his heart knocking violently against his ribs. What if he had slept on? The very thought made him feel weak and hollow inside.

During the last ten days he had slept very little. It was a mercy that today was the last exam. When he returned to his room, he would lock himself in and sleep round the clock. An ocean of soothing darkness undulated invitingly in his mind's eye, and with this he felt his tiredness returning and the burning in his eyes increasing. He pulled himself together. This was no time to relax. Taking out two scribbled sheets of paper he began to read as he rushed along, 'Nature is a kind mother. The Romantics opened men's eyes to the beauties of nature. . . .' Films of heat shook like water in the distance before him and the sun roared in his head.

Inside the examination hall it was cool and pleasant. He wiped the streaming perspiration from his face and had a drink of water, folding his palms around the cool, moist, earthenware cup. The light was mellow too—yellow electric light—as compared to the fierce sunlight outside, and the whir of electric fans and the confusion of the boys' talk seemed to fill the hall with fluttering wings. Suddenly, the clock boomed the hour of three and all sound died. The stillness buzzed in his ears and then he heard the dry rustle of examination papers being handed out.

He got his question sheet and began to read it slowly and carefully. He read it through but it did not make any sense. There was Wordsworth and nature, Keats and beauty, Shelley and love, but no sense. He read the questions again, but with no better result. A panic seized him; he was going to fail. He shut his eyes and rested his head on the desk and said to himself: 'I am tired, I just have to buckle down, this is the last exam, I can't give up.' He opened his eyes and looked around. Pens were racing eagerly over paper all around him. The concentration on the faces of the examinees frightened him.

The invigilators were standing in a bunch at the wide entrance of the hall, talking in low tones amongst themselves. Only one invigilator was floating around and he was at the far end of the hall.

Twenty minutes went by and Nasim had not written a single word. What was he to do? Unconsciously his hand travelled to his pocket and as he touched it he gave a start as if he had touched a live wire. For a few minutes he struggled, but soon his mind was made up. He must take the help of his notes. Five minutes passed. The talk of the invigilators at the entrance seemed interminable, and the one who was circulating had again drifted away to the farthest corner.

Nasim quickly drew the folded sheets from his pocket and placed them among the pages of his exam book, gave himself a little time, and began to write. He was drawing to the end of the first question when a hand was laid on his shoulder, giving him a violent shock.

'May I see your exam book?' said the invigilator. Nasim was shaking like a leaf. *It's all over* flashed in his mind. The suspended electric lights began to sway before his eyes and the huge hall rocked like a ship in a troubled sea. He swooped down towards the feet of the invigilator and touching them, said with a stifled sob, 'I touch your feet, sir; please forgive me this time. I won't do it again.'

'No, no, what are you doing?' said the man, stepping back from his outstretched hands. He helped the boy back on to his stool and, with the two confiscated sheets of paper in his possession, walked away.

In a few minutes the head invigilator came along. The boy's book was taken away and he was told to leave: 'Now you may go; you will hear from the University later.' He knew what that meant; but he was much calmer now. He rose in silence and went out like a man in a dream.

Outside, the scene had not changed. The sun was

still beating down fiercely and the hot wind brandished knives. But he felt nothing. The connection between him and the outside world seemed to have snapped. He kept on walking blindly, and when he found himself opposite the Students' Café, he went in and asked for a cup of tea. The waiter, in only a loin cloth, drowsily served him and returned behind the counter to lie down on the floor. There was nobody else. A time piece ticked in a niche and a vile smell floated in from the open drain outside; the flies buzzed and the heat was oppressive.

It was the end of everything, he thought. He would be rusticated for three years; he knew that was the rule. Three terrible vacant years, and after that, even if he won a degree, he would never be able to get a decent job with the collar of rustication around his neck. How cruelly his future had been emptied out for him! He felt a dull pain in his mind, and then, suddenly he forgot all about his crime and the terrible punishment he had brought upon himself. The heat, the buzzing flies, the sleeping waiter, the ticking clock, all receded from him, circled away.

It was a winter's evening and he was a child. He was standing by himself in a room and listening, as he had often done before. In the adjacent room his father was shouting at his mother, and when she came out she was crying. He had been waiting for her. He did not say anything but quietly went up to her and touched her dress. She put her hand on his shoulder and he flung his arms around her, burying his face in the folds of her garments. They sat down and for a long time mother and son talked, like one child to another. She complained and he listened, sitting beside her and feeling the warmth of her body.

'He's always shouting at me. At the least little thing

he gets angry. I don't ask for money for myself; there are things needed in the house . . .' and in this way she aired her grievances to the sympathetic child. 'I have never known a day's happiness in this house, always slaving, always being shouted at. You children are my only happiness. When you grow up and become a high-ranking officer and earn a lot of money, only then will I know rest and comfort.'

The nine-year-old understood all this and his eyes answered her. Then suddenly he said, 'We won't keep father.'

'Your father is not bad,' she said, 'he is only worried for want of money. He denies himself such a lot. Everything he does is for you children, and he wants to do so much.' This contradiction in his mother's feelings puzzled his child's brain.

She got up and went to the kitchen where he followed her, and, sitting by the fire, watched her cooking dinner. The kitchen was the place where she was completely at her ease, sure of everything. She would stir the steaming meat, take out a little fire-hot lentils on her palm and taste it for salt, prod the fire, wash up, and arrange the shining pots and pans in a row on the open shelf. Finally, today, she kneaded the dough and put the iron-plate on the fire. She made dough balls and, putting them on a board, rolled them out. Under the deft movements of the rolling pin they expanded into perfect circles.

He watched with interest the nimble movements of her hands and said, 'Mother, let me do it too.'

'No,' she said, 'why should you do it? It's not a man's work. When you grow up and get married, your wife will cook for you.' She paused for a moment and continued, 'No, even your wife will not cook. You will have servants. They will cook. I shall not cook either.' She stopped again and then said, 'But I shall keep an eye on the servants; they are such thieves.'

'Mother,' he said now, 'I have gone and done a terrible thing. I have shattered your dreams. I could give my life to reclaim it.' He woke from his reverie and was surprised to discover that his tears had been flowing unconsciously. He wiped his eyes. The waiter's steady snores came from behind the counter. He counted out the change on the table and left quietly without disturbing him.

The heat had lessened considerably. The University clock struck half-past five. He did not know so much time had elapsed. In another half an hour the students would be free and would come streaming out of the examination hall. The thought of facing them and talking to them scared him. His impulse was to get away quickly; there wasn't much time left.

He started walking down Fort Road, which led to the river. As the heat retreated, life crept out of its shelters. There were some pedestrians on the road and the stray cattle that had herded under the trees were shaking themselves to get up. He walked on, past the men and the cattle, past the bungalows that stood back from the road, past the stubbled fields, till he reached the old fort that Emperor Akbar had built and which the river now washed.

By now the sun had set, leaving red patches on the sky. A little away from the water's edge stood a huge peepal tree, its leaves moving in the wind like human palms from the wrist down. He bent down and picked up a handful of sand; it was warm. But the river's water was cool. He sat there a long time moving his hand in the water and drawing figures on the sand till night fell and the fields around him grew quite dark. He heard the lapping of the water, stood up, and started walking along the river. He kept walking he did not know for how long. Then a little ahead of him he saw a mighty tree standing like a gigantic shadow and beneath it was a temple. A feeble light glimmered there and occasionally someone beat on a gong. He saw a tiny spark shine in the distance on the other side of the river. He watched it. It grew into a tongue of flame. Other tongues sprang up beside it and they blended into a blaze. Then a distant wailing rose on the air.

'My God,' he said, as a terrifying fear clutched at his heart, 'who has led me to the burning-ghat?'

He retraced his steps, stumbling along in the dark, and with a frightening vividness the memory of his first days in Benares came back to him.

His father, a petty government officer, had been transferred there. As the train drew up at the station, the children jumped out with enthusiasm to see what Benares was like. They knew it was a holy city and that it was famous for its mornings. It was a pity, Nasim thought, that it was no longer morning and the broad daylight was like daylight anywhere.

Outside the station they hired tongas and were soon riding through the streets, which were crowded with hawkers, pedestrians, stray cattle, and vehicles of every description. They were held up by a long line of creaking bullock-carts. Then all of a sudden he heard, above the noise of the traffic, the cry of *'Ram Nam Sat Hei'*, the formula they repeat loudly when they carry the dead. His eyes moved in the direction of the sounds, and there it was, sure enough, a bier, carried on shoulders. His eyes fastened on it. The body was tightly strapped to a light frame of bamboo. The shape of the head and shoulders and the outline of the body were clearly visible under the vermillion shroud. Flower chains were heaped on the chest of the corpse and coloured powder stuck in patches to the winding sheet. The proximity at which the dead man passed frightened him. The bier lurched at every step with the body's weight. But soon it was out of sight. The other people had hardly noticed it. They had just made way for it as for a passing vehicle. In five minutes there was another, and yet another. The dead were a constant part of the living traffic.

'Why do so many people die here?' he asked his father in a hushed tone.

'It's a holy city. Many people who are sick and dying come here. They think that if they die here, they will go to heaven,' his father said.

'Will they?' he asked automatically.

'No, they won't. No Hindu ever goes to heaven,' his father replied.

The tongas ambled along. He had sunk into silence. He was feeling new and deeply disturbing sensations. The twelve-year-old boy had never had such an experience that had shaken him to his roots.

'There,' said his father's friend, who had received them at the station and was riding with them, 'that's your house over there.' About a hundred yards from the road was a small bungalow that had been rented for them, partly hidden from view by a grove of trees. Before they turned into the approach an *ekka* passed them. Two biers were tied to each side of it, feet forward. As the cart raced along the dead men's heads shook continuously like two giant knobs. Once again, in terrified fascination, he watched them. The gravel on the approach crunched under the steel tyres of the tongas, and they were home at last. When he got off he was cold inside. The dead were everywhere.

The day passed in great misery. A heaviness that he had never known before pressed down on him all the time. He was silent and apprehensive with premonitions of danger.

At night the beds were arranged in a double row in the open, under the sky. His mother and the younger children were in one row, he with his father and another brother in the other. His father offered his prayers before retiring, making sing-song recitations from the Quran, after which he lay down and was soon fast asleep. The silence of the night deepened, with only some small sounds coming from the trees. The sky was beautiful with the stars, which looked so distant and peaceful. But Nasim was uneasy. His unknown fear had not subsided. He turned his face towards his father, shut his eyes and silently repeated verses from the Quran to calm his mind. He told himself that nothing was the matter, but that was not true. His uneasiness did not leave him; he seemed to be anticipating danger. The summer night wore on and sleep was miles away from his eyes.

There came a gust of wind from somewhere and the dry leaves on the palm tree rattled like tin. One leaf broke off and slid down the entire length of the trunk, grating all the way. His father stirred. In a minute he got up and took a drink from the pitcher stand. When he returned, Nasim called in a feeble voice, 'Father.'

'Yes?'

'I can't sleep.'

His father brought him a glass of water, put his hand on his head and said, 'New places are sometimes like that.'

Nasim lay down, comforted and secure, and this time the night covered him like cool soft velvet and he fell asleep.

When he awoke after some time, he felt he had given a start. His heart was beating rapidly. He thought he heard those voices he had heard in the daytime in the street. He strained his ears but the night was still. He waited. And sure enough the mourning voices were there, faint and struggling at first, then clearer and stronger, as the dead man's party approached on the road. Then slowly they faded away, leaving him in a cold sweat. A little later it grew light. His father got up and said his prayers.

From that day onwards he mostly heard those voices first in his sleep on such nights. He would wake up and everything would be perfectly still, but he would wait for them with a certainty that he knew so well. Then, breaking the silence they would come, those cries of *'Ram Nam Sat Hei'*, faint and struggling at first, then louder and louder, dancing wildly and curving like a dagger on the night, and then they would gradually fade, leaving him sick and exhausted. People say that familiarity wears the edge off feelings. But he could never get familiar with the dead. After two years they were transferred from Benares.

I wonder if they would call me a coward if I told them all this now, he thought. He looked at the river which was darker than the darkness around him and thought: it will flow through Benares, the sacred city that I dreaded. It takes the dead to the sea, washing their spirits clean in the holy water. The sea must be full of ghosts. What do they do there? Sport and frolic?

He walked on and his thoughts sank below his consciousness. Lifting up his head he looked into the distance and saw someone dragging a chain of light through the darkness. It was a train passing over a bridge. He thought with pleasure that the train was capable of so much beauty. 'Everything is capable of beauty,' he said aloud, without meaning anything, and started walking towards the bridge. He was an hour getting there.

He had to climb a steep slope to get to the top and onto the bridge. From there it was a drop of some thirty feet to the river. The bridge itself was a narrow structure with no railings on either side, and even the space between the wooden sleepers, on which a single track was laid, was open. It was like a big ladder laid across the river. He stepped cautiously onto the bridge and went slowly from sleeper to sleeper. He viewed himself from a distance in his imagination: the broad river, the narrow bridge, the darkness of the night, and a solitary figure taking measured steps on it. The image pleased him immensely.

When he was midway across, he saw a pinpoint of light on the northern horizon before him. It was like a pale star, and slowly it seemed to grow into a small moon—a star leaving the depths of space and bringing light to him. He looked at it in fascination. The moon grew and grew till he could see rays coming out of it. Then there was the shriek of a whistle and he woke up to the danger he was in. It was a train coming. He turned back and retreated from sleeper to sleeper in haste, moving quickly but calmly. The train thundered on to the bridge, the sleepers shook under his feet and a flood of light fell around him and the water below sparkled. Suddenly, for a moment, it occurred to him that he heard the voices—his old voices—faint and struggling over the roar of the train. Then something hit him fiercely from behind . . . There was a splash in the river.

MOTHER

They were in the middle of their supper when the telephone rang. The boy got up to attend to it in the living room.

'Dad, it's for you, from Karachi,' he called.

Safdar Beg pushed back his chair, stood up and went to the phone. It was his sister speaking, and she was crying.

'Mother died an hour ago,' she said. 'Burial is today; *soyam* will be after three days.'

His wife and two children, eating at the kitchen table, heard his monosyllables and silences.

'What is it?' his wife enquired.

'Mother died,' he said. 'Najiba is on the phone.'

His wife repeated the Arabic formula for the departed soul to rest in peace.

Safdar was not grieved by the news. In fact, he was immensely relieved. He had prayed many times to the God he did not believe in to let his mother die. He wanted to tell his sister that it was good that Mother was no more, that at last her suffering had come to an end. She

151

had been in a coma for almost a year, and for six months before that she had been completely paralysed. She could still see then, probably without comprehension, but she could not speak or move. He wanted to tell his sister that death was a mercy, but she was crying so piteously that he could not say anything. The intensity of her grief overwhelmed his intended consolation.

When the call concluded and he put the receiver back, he did not return to his meal, but kept sitting by himself in the dark living room. The sound level in the kitchen had dropped perceptibly and the supper had ended prematurely .

In a few minutes his wife came in, bringing him a cup of tea.

'Have something to drink,' she said. 'You didn't finish your supper.' Placing the tea on the corner table, she snapped on the light. With the light his mind emerged from its hole of darkness, and he told his wife all that he could not tell his sister: how meaningless and ruthlessly tenacious the habit of living was, that it took nature almost two years to cut an aged throat, fibre by fibre. He was angry.

'Oh! How she suffered!' he said.

'Yes.'

'Why?' he demanded more loudly.

To this she made no answer. She heard his further comments also in silence. Suddenly she said, 'You should go to Karachi.'

This was out of the blue for him. 'Why?' he asked, 'she'll be buried today.'

'No, for the *soyam*,' she said.

Again his mind could not follow her reasoning.

Was he to travel to the other side of the globe just to attend a ritual prayer meeting for one dead and buried? Yet he offered no resistance to the suggestion. In fact, he readily agreed.

'All right. I'll go,' he said, and deep down in some obscure way he was pleased that he was undertaking this pointless journey.

Half an hour later, his son said, 'Your reservation is for tomorrow evening, Air Canada, Flight 601.'

'What?' he said, not by way of objection, but in surprise. First, it hadn't occurred to him that he should go to Karachi, yet he was going. Then, it didn't occur to him that all it would take to arrange his travel was to pick up the phone and, now that it had been done so promptly and easily, he was pleasantly surprised.

He had lived in Canada for twenty-five years now, a little less than half his life. He had not only accepted the ways of the new world, but had also liked them. Yet they did not come naturally to him. The telephone, for instance—he liked it, it was so convenient, yet he was uncomfortable conversing with a disembodied voice. It was like talking to a doorknob or to a piece of furniture. He would rather talk face to face with people. The same applied to the English language, which he used most of the time. He could handle it well. His class inspection reports were good; so were the evaluations done by his students. But he knew that English had failed to be incarnated in him. It was a tool of his mind, not a limb.

The next morning, at the college, he was in for another surprise. He could not have anticipated the reaction of the head of the department. He had thought that when he told him he would be away for a whole week

153

in mid-term, the chairman would not like it and a shadow of annoyance would pass over his face. He was going away like this for the second time in sixteen months—first when Mother was taken ill, and now when she had died. But old Fletcher did not react like that at all. Instead, he was sincerely sorry and sympathetic.

'Take ten days off,' he said. 'You don't have to run up to there and rush back immediately. Spend some time with your family. We'll look after your classes and the lab.'

In the evening he was on the plane. He had brought some class work along with him, but his mind would not focus on it. It wandered off to thoughts of Mother.

She had brought on her illness herself by staging a kind of medieval play in the inner courtyard of the house. One of her sons, an eminent Karachi surgeon, had gone to London to attend a medical conference and also to have a medical check-up. He had been having chest pains and he had a lot of doctor friends there from his medical-student days, some of whom were well-known cardiologists now.

He was to come back in a week's time. But the doctors found his heart arteries badly clogged and advised immediate by-pass surgery. That delayed his return. Mother asked why he wasn't back, in answer to which an excuse was made: he was looking into some research in his field of work. But as the days went by, she grew uneasy.

'You are hiding something from me,' she said, which, of course, was denied.

On the day set for the surgery she either had a premonition of danger or read the expression on the faces around her. She was sitting on the divan in the verandah next to her *pandan,* when all of a sudden she jumped up and ran barefooted and bareheaded out into the courtyard. Her hands were stretched out like a mendicant's, and her *dopatta,* which she had snatched from her head and shoulders, was draped over her extended arms, with the slack in the middle forming a kind of begging bowl. Her face was lifted to the sky and she was hysterically crying: 'Lord, have pity on my child. Take my life; do anything to punish me, but spare my son.'

The outburst brought everyone racing out of their rooms.

'Mother, what are you doing?' cried Najiba, as she flung her arms around her.

'It's my son's life,' she moaned.

'Rashid *Bhai* is all right,' said Najiba, and led her back to the verandah. Mother took a few unsteady steps, collapsed and fainted.

There was even greater commotion now, and she was rushed to the hospital. The doctors said she had burst a brain vessel.

She did not regain consciousness for two days. On the third day she revived and stammered out: 'How is he?'

'He is all right,' she was told and it was explained that he had had open-heart surgery which went very well.

'Lord, I thank you a million times,' she murmured, 'a hundred million times.' Then she closed her eyes and went back to sleep.

When she woke the next day, her speech was gone. She could open her eyes and see, but could not say a word. The first stroke was quickly followed by a series of strokes until she lost the use of all her limbs.

In November, Safdar had flown to Karachi to see her. He found her sitting, propped up in her hospital bed. There was infinite sadness in her eyes. They looked steadily at him, but there was not a glimmer of recognition in them.

'Mother, it's me, Safdar.'

Not a flicker.

'Don't you recognize me?' he asked.

Nothing.

He broke down and sobbed like a child, with his head on her lap. There was no response on her part of any kind. He raised his head. The eyes were the same in their deep sadness.

'I hope that she doesn't know me,' he said to himself. 'I pray she doesn't know what is happening to her.'

The doctors said she had lost comprehension. But he was not sure. Why that sadness? Was she a helpless witness to her own crucifixion?

When they were driving back home from the hospital, Safdar was silent, anguished and angry.

'What kind of a God is this,' he was saying to himself, 'who uses a distraught woman's words as a licence to do this?' But later, in calmer moments, he said, 'How can I blame a God in whose existence I don't believe?' And this see-saw of emotional and rational moods was repeated many times in the months that followed.

The second day after his arrival, his youngest sister reached Karachi from Belgium. She had a child, two-years of age. The family took him along with them when they went to the hospital in the evening. Safdar noticed that when his mother's eyes rested on the child, the sadness lifted from them. He marvelled at the change.

The next day, the boy was naughty. He repeated a swear word in her presence that one of his uncles had taught him by way of fun. Mother openly smiled at this.

It was important after that to take him to the hospital every day. Safdar wondered: does she know who the child is? Probably not. Does she know who she herself is? Probably not. Probably it was the eternal woman responding to the eternal child when the level of individual personalities had been erased.

He returned to Toronto, but the news of Mother's steady deterioration continued to reach him. Soon, the eternal woman's response was gone too. Mother closed her eyes, never to open them again. Now she lived at the level of physical reflexes only. They would open her mouth and put a bolus of soft food in it, and the gullet would automatically gulp it down.

He was no longer interested in her life. He only wished for her death as the fear haunted him that sometimes, in that mindless sleep, her consciousness flickered to a flame and she saw herself entombed in her own body, suffocating, dying, but still alive.

'Please die, Mother,' he would say, and at such moments he hated God.

The plane touched down at Karachi.

One of his nephews met him at the airport. They did not talk as they drove back. The boy had begun, 'Grandma was found dead in bed.'

No answer from him.

'She had shrunk to half her size, a skeleton covered with skin.'

157

No answer.

There was silence after that. He was glad that he was not present at the funeral and had not seen her grotesque transformation.

They left the highway and were passing through residential streets. Against the drab walls of the houses the morning light looked dirty. It was hot; he rolled down the window on his side. Whiffs of foul odour hit his nostrils from time to time. There was not much traffic at this early hour. But the stray dogs were there in plenty, nosing around. One was almost run over by them. There was a screech of brakes and a jolt that shook him badly. Hens were out too, scratching on the little mounds of garbage left along the roadside. In this chaotic and crowded assault on his senses, his mind felt fatigued and he longed for the sensuous frugality and orderly impressions of Toronto.

'This city needs to be put through a wash,' he thought in his depression, 'a car wash.'

The *soyam* was a well-attended function. Some four hundred people were present: men in the large tent on the spacious grounds of the doctor's residence, women inside the house. These were relatives, family friends and sympathetic strangers who had read in the papers about the service for the dead and wanted to be a part of it. Separately bound chapters of the Quran were handed out which the guests circulated amongst themselves. The more times the holy book was finished, the more credit would be accrued for the departed soul to help it in its difficult passage to the eternal world. When the scriptural reading was done, there was tea, refreshments and socializing.

Safdar ran into his cousin, a professor of Islamic law at the University of Karachi.

'*Assalaam-alaikum, Bhai* Safdar,' said Rizwan.

'Hello, Rizwan,' responded Safdar.

'Your mother's soul will be pleased that you came all the way from Canada to pray for her,' said his cousin.

As if refusing to be comforted, Safdar replied, 'I don't think, Rizwan, that it matters the least little bit to the dead whether we pray or don't pray for them. They have no interest in what we do. In fact, they have no interest in either life or death. Life and death are preoccupations of the living only. We do all these things,' he continued, waving his hands around, 'for our own peace of mind, especially if death makes a kill within our view.'

'You mean our prayers cannot reach the world of spirits?' queried Rizwan.

'No, I mean there is no world of spirits,' replied Safdar.

'Oh,' said his cousin, 'then where do souls of the dead go?'

'Where does the flame of the candle go when the candle is burnt out?' Safdar asked.

'Ah,' said Rizwan, 'an interesting idea, but not relevant.'

'How so?'

'A good piece of reasoning, only you have left an important factor out of the account—faith,' said his cousin.

'I have left all fantasies out of the account,' Safdar replied.

'But,' said Rizwan, 'faith is not a fantasy. It is one of the solid realities of our life. It anchors the mind to the immovable Spirit, so that it may not flounder in the sea of

159

ceaseless change. The sea washes over it, but it remains
secure. The unattached mind would be at the mercy of the
waves, drifting, bobbing and crashing against the shore.
Without faith in the world of the spirit, life would be a
continual anxiety, full of fear and empty of meaning.'

'But that is exactly what real life is as opposed to
your self-induced hypnosis and open disregard of facts,'
Safdar replied.

'Where does the soul come from?' asked Rizwan,
to make a proper beginning again.

'From the body,' said Safdar, 'like the bud of light
that comes out of the candle.'

'You have lived too long in the West,' said his
cousin. 'For me the spiritual world is self-evidently there
and the encroachments of reason cannot enter into it, like
flies buzzing outside a window-pane. But I like your "bud
of light"; it's a good image.'

'Your "flies" is not bad either.'

Mother also believed absolutely in the world of
spirits, as did her mother before her. Safdar often recalled
with amusement a conversation between his mother and
grandmother which he had overheard when he was a boy
of ten.

'Daughter, did you hear what she said?'

'Who? Who said what?'

'Your grandmother.' (She had been dead for five
years.)

'What did she say?'

'She came in my dream last night and said, "I am
cold"'.

Safdar's grandmother used to make ten quilts
every winter and distribute them among the poor as a

spiritual help to her late mother. That year she had forgotten to do it. Hence the visit and the reminder.

A bale of cotton was bought the same day and a 'cotton-thrasher' sent for—one of the favourite characters of Safdar's childhood. The man came with his bow slung across his shoulder and his wooden dumb-bell in his hand. He undid the bale, broke up the compressed material into lumps, put his bow-string in the middle of a lump on the floor, and started making his music by plucking the string with his dumb-bell. The string vibrating in the cotton separated the fibres from one another. The whole day Safdar could hear the bow going tin-tin-tin-twang, tin-tin-tin-twang. He would sometimes push the door open and see what was going on. Yes, the man was there strumming his bow, sitting in a white fog of flying cotton, his mouth and nose covered with a scarf, and his head and eyebrows snowy with the white fibres that had settled on them. By evening, the small mass of compact cotton had been converted into a soft, fleecy, white mountain. The next day five young women were called from the poor quarters. These excellent seamstresses stuffed and stitched the quilts and by sundown they reached the needy families.

Both the worlds, the transient one of flesh and blood and the permanent one of the spirit, were ruled by God. He was the sole, undisputed and all-powerful lord and master of everything that there was. This was Mother's unshakable belief and the fountain of her existence. The other great reality of her life was her love for her children. She could not love her husband for he would not allow it. Both he and she were brought up in a cultural environment in which the husband had the position of lord and master and the role of the wife was obedience to this earthly god.

In Mother's mind, only God was lord and master. She knew that if someone sleeps with a woman then he has a weakness and cannot be a god, no matter how hard he pretends to be one in the daytime. Of course, she never rebelled against his authority; that was unthinkable. But their relationship, in spite of its correct appearance, was hollow and artificial. There were no joys of true intimacy, no moments of two personalities merging into each other to form a richer and higher one. There were only two separate persons, with one dominating and using the other.

The children imposed no such conditions on her love. They accepted whatever she gave, and she gave them all she had, her entire self, more than her self. Her love was ecstatic.

Mother was well content to live her life by these two profound truths until one day they collided and nearly shattered her mind. Safdar's youngest brother, Firoze, a gorgeous youth of twenty-three, died suddenly. He left home in the morning to go to the Air Force base—a happy, laughing lad—and four hours later came back a mangled corpse in a military ambulance. There had been a crash.

Mother was frantic with grief. She tore her hair, beat her head against the wall, and raised piercing cries to high heaven. She had to be injected with a sedative to calm her down.

Her husband, himself a devout Muslim, but of the stern type, had also shaken like a leaf when the boy's body was brought in, but he did not shed a tear or raise a cry. He went groping like a blind man to his prayer carpet, sat

162

down and raising both his hands kept repeating: 'He was yours, O God. You gave him to us, we took him with open arms. Now you have taken him back and we submit to your will.'

But Mother was inconsolable for weeks. Her tears would not stop flowing. When her husband told her of God and submission to His will, she wailed in her agony: 'I submit! I submit! But what am I to do with my mother's heart?'

The tears did dry up in a few months, but the sighs continued to the end of her life, for thirteen years. 'He's angry with me,' she would say of her dead son, sighing like the wind going through a ruin. 'He has never come in my dream. He has come to others, but never to me. I cried too much. God did not like it. This is my punishment. I did a disservice to my Firoze.' And remorsefully she would relate the contents of poet Iqbal's 'A Mother's Dream'.

In this poem a mother wakes up in her dream in a dark and dismal country. She has never seen a place like this before. She looks around and sees a chain of light moving in the murky distance. She advances towards it and finds it is a procession of children going somewhere, with each child holding a tiny torch in his hand to guide his immediate steps. The youngster bringing up the rear is having problems. His torch has gone out and he is lagging behind. She approaches the straggler and recognizes him to be her lately deceased son. She runs to him, embraces him, and then complains about his deserting her and how she cries day and night for him. On hearing this the child averts his face and says, 'I know you cry, but that hasn't done me any good. See, how your tears have put out my

163

light.'

It was probably to avoid making this mistake again that Mother rushed recklessly into the awful presence of the Mighty Judge and pleaded for a substitution. And before the sword could fall on her second son, she threw herself between the divine stroke and the victim and was herself cut in two.

Of course, Safdar in his sane moments did not believe a word of this version of the event, but, at the same time, he could not shake off the idea once and for all. It lingered in the shadows of his mind and jumped into the light whenever the opportunity arose.

On his last day in Karachi, he went to his mother's grave. Sprinkling water and strewing flowers over it, he said, 'The earth will rest lightly on you, Mother, and no one will be able to hurt you any more, not even your God.'

On his return flight his mood was one of quiet buoyancy. He did not talk much with his fellow passengers, but inwardly he was at peace. He read half a book and had a few drinks. Flying over the Atlantic, as they approached the Canadian coast, he pulled a travel brochure from the back-pocket of the seat in front of him and started turning over its pages. On the centre pages there was a route map of the airlines—firm black lines curving gracefully over brown and green land and blue seas, joining one point to another.

It was a beautiful pattern. Suddenly, it flashed in his mind that this was the travel map of his mother's spiritual world, of souls bound for different destinations, going to cities of heaven and towns of hell, to enchanted sunny islands of the blessed and gloomy muddy lagoons of the damned.

There was a sudden lurch as the plane hit an airpocket and he was almost thrown out of his seat. The fasten-seat-belt sign came on. He strapped himself securely and looked out of the window. They were flying through a cloud, which seemed to go on and on endlessly. After ten minutes or so he began to feel dizzy. He felt that the cloud had begun pouring in at the window, and as it filled the plane it blotted out everything from his view. There were no other passengers. He was alone, rushing through a fog. His eyes were open, he could see, but his space had no horizon on which he could mark directions and destinations. He knew he was going but did not know where, and he thought: what if this journey through nothing to nowhere lasted for ever?

It was at this point that he cried out in panic, 'Why have you left me alone?'

An air-hostess, a woman in her thirties who had spoken with him earlier, came running to his seat and shook his shoulders. His vision slowly returned, and he said to her, 'Why had you left me alone?'

'We didn't leave you alone,' she stated simply.

'Where are we going?'

'We are going to Toronto,' she replied. 'You live there, don't you? We are going home. Probably you had a bad dream. Wait, I'll go and get you a drink.'

While she was gone, his mind returned to his experience and he said to himself, 'So, this was what Pascal felt, the terror of modern space when science replaced the secure religious universe held in the arms of God with this scary, endless, meaningless extension in which one is lost as in a nightmare. . . .'

The air-hostess returned with the drink. 'Here,'

she offered. 'Have this. You'll feel better.'

He took the glass, had a sip, smiled sheepishly, and, to hide the embarrassment he felt at having created a scene, said, 'Tell Mr. Pascal to fly in the other space, in the clear blue sky, above the clouds.'

'Mr. Pascal?' she asked gently.

'The pilot. Isn't he the pilot?'

'No. Captain Johnson is the pilot.'

Because she looked worried, he hastened to add, 'I'm sorry. That was just a joke.'

'Who is Pascal, anyway?' she asked.

'Oh, him? He's a Frenchman, a seventeenth-century Frenchman, the first man to recognize the nature of secular space.'

'Secular space?' she echoed, looking puzzled.

'It's the scary one,' he replied. 'The other one is Mother's space.'

'Oh,' she said, her face brightening. 'I get it. Like mother's cooking?'

'Exactly,' he said, and both of them laughed.

'You are a funny man, Mr. Beg.'

'I guess I am.'

Before she left, she put her hand on his shoulder in a good-natured way. 'Next time we are lost in a cloud, I'll bring you a drink right away.'

'That will be fine,' he said.

Printed in Canada